S

"Will you join me?"

"If you want me to."

She stepped closer to him. "I'd like that...husband."

He took a step back. "This isn't going to be a marriage in the romantic sense, Rosalind. Just so we're clear on that."

"I'm perfectly well aware of our situation. Now, do you want to bathe with me or not?"

In response, he shrugged off his jacket and his hands went to the tie at his neck, unknotting it and yanking it from under his collar. Next, he undid the buttons of his shirt. Steam quickly began to fog the window behind them. Ros found herself mesmerized by the play of muscles across his back as he bent and swirled something fragrant and foamy in the water.

When he stood and returned to her, she was still frozen in place. Caught by the beauty of this man—this stranger—whom she'd married.

* * *

Married by Contract by
Yvonne Lindsay is part of the
Texas Cattleman's Club: Fathers and Sons series.

Dear Reader,

I am honored to be a part of this series of stories and to work with the amazing authors who are also contributing.

Wealthy cattle rancher Gabriel Carrington is a cautious man who's been burned by both family and love. He's done with romance but dearly desires a child of his own to love, without the complications of a traditional marriage. He's employed the services of a professional matchmaker to meet a like-minded woman who doesn't mind having access to his money while providing him with the son or daughter he's always wanted. He isn't, in any way, looking for love.

Rosalind Banks, a successful Australian fashion designer, believes in love and happy-ever-after. When she and Gabe meet and pour out their woes to one another, they develop a powerful mutual attraction—one that leads to a heated night of passion, and that night leads to the one thing Gabe most wants in the world: a baby. So what does he propose? Well, marriage of course, but not the kind that Rosalind always dreamed of.

Will they find happiness, or are they destined to failure?

Best wishes,

Yvonne Lindsay

YvonneLindsay.com

YVONNE LINDSAY

MARRIED BY CONTRACT

Special thanks and acknowledgment are given to Yvonne Lindsay for her contribution to the Texas Cattleman's Club: Fathers and Sons miniseries.

Recycling programs for this product may not exist in your area.

ISBN-13: 978-1-335-73534-8

Married by Contract

This edition published by arrangement with Harlequin Books S.A.

For questions and comments about the quality of this book, please contact us at CustomerService@Harlequin.com.

Harlequin Enterprises ULC
22 Adelaide St. West, 41st Floor
Toronto, Ontario M5H 4E3, Canada
www.Harlequin.com

Printed in U.S.A.

Award-winning author **Yvonne Lindsay** is a *USA TODAY* bestselling author of more than forty-five titles with over five million copies sold worldwide. Always having preferred the stories in her head to the real world, Yvonne balances her days crafting the stories of her heart or planting her nose firmly in someone else's book. You can reach Yvonne through her website, yvonnelindsay.com.

Books by Yvonne Lindsay

Harlequin Desire

Clashing Birthrights

Seducing the Lost Heir
Scandalizing the CEO
What Happens at Christmas...

Texas Cattleman's Club: Fathers and Sons

Married by Contract

Visit her Author Profile page at Harlequin.com, or yvonnelindsay.com, for more titles.

You can find Yvonne Lindsay on Facebook, along with other Harlequin Desire authors, at Facebook.com/harlequindesireauthors!

I dedicate this to all the dreamers and lovers out there. May all your endings be happy.

One

November

"What do you mean they canceled the order?" Rosalind mentally calculated the time back in Sydney, Australia, where Piers was calling from, and schooled herself to remain calm. "They can't simply cancel like that."

"They can and they did, Ros. They're citing long-term fallout from the pandemic and a need to cut back. I'm sorry—they see our product as being luxury driven at a time when people are being more careful with household expenditure. The arm of this thing is long. We both know that."

Her operations manager, Piers Benet, sounded

calm, but then again, he'd had several hours to come to terms with the news that could easily derail Rosalind's entire business.

"Did you point out to them they signed the contract after the start of the pandemic?"

"I did, but they're cutting us loose. We get to keep the first payment, though, so there's that."

It was small consolation compared to the full contract value, not to mention the value of the exposure of her fashion label into every one of Australia's major department stores or her production costs to date.

"So, there's nothing we can do?" she said bitterly, pacing her hotel room.

"Nothing except hope your contacts in New York give us the uptake we need to remain afloat. How are things in New York, anyway?"

"I'm not actually in New York yet."

"You're not? Is there a problem?"

"No, not really. I…uh…thought I'd call in, say hi to Drake."

"Drake Rhodes? That Drake?"

Piers knew the full extent of the brief but fierce relationship she'd had with the Texan billionaire businessman during his six months in Sydney and he also knew that she'd walked away from Drake when he'd made it clear he was not into marriage. Wanting more than accepting happy-for-now, Rosalind had reluctantly ended their liaison when he'd had to fly home to Royal because his half-sister was ill.

But time had given her a new perspective and she was willing to give them both another chance. It was why she was here in Royal, Texas, staying at the Bellamy, instead of already being in New York. A selfish choice, maybe, especially when her business currently teetered on a knife edge, but a necessary one. She had to know if she'd made the right decision because she could never forgive herself if she'd walked away from him too soon.

She couldn't quite believe that Drake had forsaken the busyness of Sydney and the exciting lifestyle they'd led there, to return to this small, so very *country* town. She knew that before he'd come to Sydney he'd lived in New York and she couldn't understand why he'd returned to his birthplace—a town he'd never spoken highly of. It made no sense to her that he'd come back here.

"Yes, that Drake," she said carefully. She knew Piers wouldn't be impressed.

"Are you sure about this, Ros? You were pretty upset when you broke up. Last thing you need right now is more emotional upheaval."

"I'll be fine," she responded firmly. "I can't help feeling I pushed him too hard, too early, on marriage. Maybe that was a mistake and all he needed was a little more time. Look, if things don't work out then I'll carry on to New York regardless. But I have to know, Piers. I can't live with 'what if' echoing in the back of my mind, forever."

Her operations manager sighed heavily on the

other end of the call. "You take care. And let me know how it goes, okay?"

"I will. And send through the report on the loss we have to carry on that order cancellation. Looks like we're going to need get creative to shift that stock. Get one of the team to look into pop-up stores in both Australia and New Zealand, okay?"

By the time they ended the call, Rosalind was beside herself with frustration. This was to have been their big break. It had meant everything to her. Sure, she was American born but she'd lived half her life in Australia and taking the Australian leisure-wear market by storm would have been the fulfilment of a childhood dream.

Rosalind flicked a glance at the diamond-encrusted Cartier watch that adorned her wrist. It had been a gift from Drake for her birthday. Tonight she'd hoped it would bring her luck for what she had planned. Winning him back.

It was time to get ready for the gala at the Texas Cattleman's Club here in Royal. She'd been lucky to get a ticket at such late notice, but she knew Drake would be there and hopefully the knockout scarlet gown she'd packed would surprise him enough to agree to them taking a second chance on each other. After Piers's phone call, she needed some good news.

Housekeeping had steamed the gown for her earlier in the day and it hung in splendor in the bedroom of her suite. Rosalind took her time over her toilette and makeup. She smoothed on lightly scented body lotion with long strokes and applied her makeup with a practiced hand to emphasize her sculpted cheekbones and large blue eyes. She'd chosen to wear her long blond hair loose, but had curled it to give it more volume and bounce and, after brushing it out and spritzing with a light mist of hair spray, she was ready to don her gown.

The deep V of the crossover front of the bodice made it impossible for her to wear a bra and she felt a shiver of excitement course through her as her nipples brushed against the lining of the dress. The V wasn't salacious, but it certainly displayed more of her lightly tanned skin than her usual attire. The lower section of the dress hugged her hips and split at the left front, exposing her leg to lower thigh as she walked.

After slipping on her silver strappy heels, she took stock of her image in the full-length mirror on the wall. Yes, she thought with a nod at her reflection, she would most definitely do just fine tonight. Now all she had to do was knock Drake's socks off, and maybe a few other items of clothing along the way, and life could resume a better normal again.

When her bedside phone chimed with a message to say her car was waiting for her, Rosalind grabbed the faux silver fur coat she knew she'd need on this cold November night and slung it over her shoulders before picking up her silver clutch and heading for the door. Tonight had to work out. Given what was happening to her business right now, she couldn't handle another failure.

There was quite a crush in the ballroom at the club when she arrived and Rosalind felt a minor quiver of trepidation as she left her coat at the coat check and made her way to where everyone was gathered. Everyone was listening to the speeches and presentations to the first responders.

A passing waiter offered a tray loaded with champagne flutes and she lifted a glass with a smile of thanks, taking a moment to sip the wine and survey the room. She searched for a familiar dark head and broad shoulders. Drake was the kind of man who dominated the room and, to be honest, there were many other men here who also fit that bill. Both dark haired and fair and all darned attractive.

"Must be something in the water," she muttered under her breath.

"The water you say? I could have sworn that was champagne."

A deep and melodic voice from right next to her made Rosalind start. She turned toward the man and took in the humor reflected in his dark, almost black, eyes. And look at that, she thought, here was another ridiculously handsome, commanding specimen. Rosalind felt an unwelcome twinge of interest. A purely instinctive feminine response to an attractive, healthy male, she told herself. She wasn't interested in anyone here but Drake, but that didn't mean she couldn't appreciate a fine-looking man when she saw one.

"I was making an observation," she said and took another sip of her wine.

"First sign of madness, you know."

"What?"

"Talking to yourself. Or so they say."

"What do *they* know?" Rosalind responded.

"Indeed. I'm Gabriel Carrington. You're not from around here, are you?"

She took the proffered hand and felt that spark of interest flame to life as his broad, warm palm connected with hers.

"Rosalind Banks, and no, I'm not."

"Ah, a woman who doesn't feel the need to inform a total stranger of every detail about herself. Sensible," he commented as he let her hand go again. "Are you visiting Royal?"

She nodded. She had no idea if her plan would work. If it did, she might be here a short while before returning to New York where hopefully Drake would join her because he'd made the bustling, vibrant East Coast city the base for all his business interests prior to his time in Sydney. If it didn't, she'd be on the next plane out of the area tomorrow and connecting to a flight to New York on her own.

"Business, or pleasure?"

"Oh, pleasure, at least I hope so," she said with a small smile.

"Then I wish you luck," he said. "It's very nice meeting you, Rosalind."

"And you," she said, raising her glass in a small toast as he raised his whiskey glass in return.

She turned her gaze back to the crowd of men in black tie and women in a dazzling array of jewel-toned evening wear. With the speeches finished, the dance floor started to fill with couples. Through the throng Rosalind caught a glimpse of a very familiar profile. Drake. He was here. She felt her body alternately ease with relief that she'd found him, and tense in anticipation of what would come next. What would he say when she told him she'd made a terrible mistake and that she wanted a second chance? There was only one way to find out and that was to approach him but she wasn't about to cut in while he was dancing. No, she'd keep her sights on him and wait until he left the floor. Then she'd make her move.

Ros turned her attention to the woman he danced with. Tall and slender with beautiful red hair and delicately fair skin, she was dressed in a couture gown of dark forest green silk that complemented her skin tone perfectly. Low cut in the front and the back and held up with spaghetti straps that showcased her feminine shoulders and with sparkling beads decorating the edges and catching the light as she moved, she was quite a vision of perfection. Ros mentally costed the gown while appreciating its cut and construction at the same time. Definitely quality and class.

The couple turned, and Ros caught a glimpse of

the woman's left hand which was adorned with a large diamond ring. She felt ice water run in her veins a moment before she schooled herself to consider that Drake may simply be dancing with a friend. Just because he was dancing with the redhead, it didn't mean they were an item, let alone an engaged item.

"See someone you know?" Gabriel Carrington asked.

He was still here?

"Yes," she said. "Over there, with the woman in the green dress."

"Drake? You know him?"

Intimately. "We met when he was in Sydney," she replied.

"Small world, huh? You're Australian."

"Australian American, to be more accurate."

"But you grew up Down Under, right? Your accent?"

She nodded, her eyes riveted on the subject of her entire reason for being here.

"Did you hear about their engagement?" Gabriel gestured toward the couple with his whiskey tumbler. "Took us all a little by surprise. Drake never made any secret about not wanting to settle down and start a family and yet, here he is."

The ice-cold sensation in her veins returned and Rosalind's hand shook a little as she lifted her champagne and downed it. Could tonight get any worse?

First the news about her business and now she was too late with Drake, as well?

"No," she finally managed. "I didn't. Have they been engaged long?"

"Not long. Here, let me get you another of those."

Gabriel took her glass and gestured to a nearby waiter who immediately came over with a replacement. Gabe pressed the glass into her hand.

"Do you want to congratulate the happy couple?" he asked.

Ros noticed that Drake and his fiancée were leaving the dance floor. They were totally absorbed in one another. She clenched her teeth as Drake bent his head and whispered something in his fiancée's ear—something that made her blush delicately before they eased their way through the crowd and out the door.

"Not particularly," she bit out, before taking another long drink of her wine.

"Ah, like that, huh?"

She turned and looked at him. "He didn't know I was coming and doesn't know I'm here. I'd prefer to keep it that way."

"Noted. Shall we move somewhere a little more private?"

"Please."

He took her by the elbow and guided her to a smaller bar area with secluded seating spaces and settled her at a table.

"You okay?" he asked.

"I will be, eventually."

She had already dealt with the disappointment of losing Drake once and, to be honest, she hadn't really thought this through enough. She should have done more research before diverting to this out-of-nowhere town with too many cows and not enough bright lights.

"Good to know. Life sucks, right?"

"Sure does. I didn't think Drake would take up with someone else quite so quickly. I had hoped..."

"Hoped?"

"That I could convince him that we deserved another chance."

"What happened?"

She finished her second glass of champagne and gestured to a waiter for another.

"I wanted love, marriage and happy-ever-after. He didn't. Not with me, anyway."

Gabriel made a sound that was a mix of irony and humor.

"What you wanted is vastly overrated. In fact, I don't think it truly exists anymore."

"Why are *you* so skeptical?" she asked, suddenly genuinely interested in the man sitting beside her.

"People only really let you see what they want you to see. It's never the truth."

"Never?"

He shook his head. "My dad cheated on my mom more times than I could count. It broke her heart. And I guess I'm more like her than I thought because the woman I thought I loved cheated on me, too. It was enough of a wake-up call for me to realize that love and happy-ever-after are merely a construct of an industry dead set on selling fake dreams."

Okay. She could see why he was so cynical. Life had a way of screwing with you. It had certainly screwed with her today.

"I think you're probably right. I guess I should have expected this with Drake. It's pretty much the icing on the cake of my shitty day so far."

"Oh?"

She drank a little more champagne. Yes, she was definitely feeling a little buzzed. It was a good feeling. It loosened her inhibitions and made her feel things she normally kept tightly controlled. It was a feeling she vastly preferred to acknowledging the fact that she was now holding on to her business by a fraying thread and her plans for her romantic future had been crushed in Royal's dust.

"Before I came out tonight, I received news that a business partner canceled their contract. We're down the tubes for close to a million bucks."

She shuddered a little. It wasn't until she'd actually admitted the true position out loud that it fully sank in.

Gabriel whistled long and low. "That's quite a hefty sum."

"Yeah, I need a cash injection and quickly, or my creditors will be baying for my blood."

"You know, it's a shame you're after the love-

and-happy-ever-after thing because marriage to me would take care of your financial problems."

She reeled a little in shock. Marriage? To him? How had they progressed to that? She'd obviously had more champagne than she'd thought because she couldn't possibly have heard that right. Still, curiosity made her press him for more.

"Marriage to you? Explain."

"I want an heir—what man doesn't—but I don't want the mess that comes with it."

"Mess? What, like love?"

He raised his glass in a toast. "You got it."

"So, what are you planning? A surrogate or something?"

"I'm not averse to marriage entirely. I see what I want as more of a business arrangement based on physical compatibility and mutual respect. There's no reason why it wouldn't work. In fact, I've employed a specialist agency to find me just the right woman. Once we marry, she gets a settlement and, when my wife gives me the heir I want, she gets unfettered access to my wealth for as long as we're married. Simple."

Rosalind let her gaze roam over him. Thick, dark hair that curled slightly, but which was tamed by an expensive haircut. Broad shoulders and a handsome face dominated by dark, intelligent eyes. A full lower lip that was perfect for nibbling on. Whoa, where did that come from? But then she let her mind wander. She'd had it with love and disappointment. Not just today but before today, too. Here she was—still single and still fighting her own battles. A bit of financial help would be nice about now. Help without a hefty personal price tag.

"And do you plan to try before you buy this new wife of yours?"

He laughed and she felt something knot up tight deep in her gut before unraveling in a heated spiral of need. He really was easy on the eyes. And a girl could get drunk on that laugh. Mind you, she was heading that way already, wasn't she, and that was probably why she formulated her next words the way she did. She was the woman scorned, in both business and in her personal life. She demanded validation to soothe her wounded soul. Gabriel Carrington was hopefully the man to provide it.

"Maybe we're both what we need after all," she said with a smile and an arch of her brow. "Tonight at least."

Two

Gabe looked at the beautiful woman sitting by him and felt every cell in his body spring to attention. Logic told him that this would be a very bad idea. She'd come here to Royal to rekindle her relationship with Drake, a man he knew and respected, and in the face of what she'd said, they'd been a serious item back in Australia. Serious enough to make her think she still had a chance with him.

That made him second-best tonight and that did not sit comfortably with him at all. And then there was her openly avowed wish for love and happy-ever-after. He wasn't in the market for that, at all. In fact, tomorrow he was meeting his latest match.

It was half the reason he had nursed a sum total

of two whiskies on ice all night long. He needed a clear head for that meeting and if the woman proved to be a promising candidate, he sure as hell didn't want to scare her off by being hungover. No woman wanted a drunk for a husband and no child deserved one as a father, either.

Which left him with a difficult decision to make. The very beautiful Ms. Rosalind Banks was sending him all the right signals. She clearly wasn't in this for complications. So how wrong would it be to take advantage of what she was so carefully suggesting? He'd never made a habit of one-night stands. He respected both himself and his prospective partners too much to simply indulge whenever the whim took him. In fact, his cast-iron control was one of the things he was most proud of. Watching what his father's infidelities had done to his mom had been more than enough to drive home the message that casual sex could be very damaging to all concerned. But both he and Rosalind had needs and he had absolutely no doubt in his mind that they'd each fulfil those needs more than adequately.

"I apologize if my forwardness has offended you," Rosalind said as his protracted silence thickened the air between them.

"No, not at all," he replied.

"We Aussies can be a bit blunt at times, I guess. Although, it generally gets us what we want, or at least leaves us knowing exactly where we stand."

"I've been accused of being blunt a time or two, myself," Gabe replied.

He liked this woman. Not only physically attractive but she was straight up, too. Not like so many women he'd met and certainly not like his cheating fiancée Francine.

"I am sorry," she apologetically. "I should probably get to my hotel."

"No, don't go. I'm not at all offended. In fact, if anything I think we should dance."

Rosalind looked at him in surprise, a slow smile pulling her luscious lips into a delicious curve. She caught her lower lip between perfectly even, white teeth and bit down firmly, as if considering what he said carefully.

"Dance, you say?"

"We could see how well we move together," he answered with a smile and a quirk of one eyebrow.

Rosalind put down her champagne glass and stood, smoothing her gown over her curves. He could not help but appreciate the fine lines of her body. At the very least, tonight should prove interesting, he thought. Gabe rose to his feet and put out one hand.

"Shall we?" he asked.

She took his hand and he laced his fingers through hers before leading the way back into the ballroom. Her hand felt tiny in his much larger one and if he wasn't mistaken her fingers trembled slightly. Anticipation, he wondered, or regret at her bold suggestion. No doubt he would soon find out. The band played a slow two-step number and Gabe pulled her into his arms. She came willingly, with one small hand resting on his shoulder and the other clasped within his own. With his other hand at the curve of her waist, he guided her onto the floor.

They moved in perfect synchronization together. It was as if they had danced this way many times before. The crowd around them melted away from his consciousness as his sole focus concentrated on the woman in his arms. They could have been anywhere, anytime. He had found her attractive on first sight, but being together like this lit a flame of desire in him that demanded an answer. As her pelvis brushed against his he increased the pressure of his hand in the small of her back encouraging her to step closer. The tremor in her fingers had stopped, but as she felt the unmistakable evidence of his arousal her small hand tightened in his and her gaze flicked up to his face.

"I'm tempted to quote a very famous movie line right now," she said with a gleam in her eye. "But I'm pretty sure I know what the answer is."

He smiled back at her and smoothly changed step as the band eased into a livelier tune. Again, in perfect sync, she adjusted seamlessly to the new steps and they continued around the dance floor. If they moved like this in public, how much better would they be in private?

Gabe nodded to Jackson Michaels as he danced past him and his partner on the crowded floor, and considered the discussion they had had earlier before the formal section of this evening. Jackson had called him out on his hunt for the perfect wife. While he hadn't given Jackson an answer one way or another, he could see the cogs moving in his friend's mind as his gaze slid over Rosalind and back to Gabe. The short nod of approval made Gabe grin broadly in response and he turned his attention back to his dance partner.

"What's so funny?" Rosalind asked.

"A friend was asking me earlier about my marital plans and I think he just gave you a tick of approval."

"And do you, too?"

"Perhaps we should consider your try-before-you-buy suggestion, first."

She missed a step and stiffened slightly before recovering smoothly. "Perhaps we should," she said looking up from beneath hooded eyelids.

It was such a sultry look that the flame that had started earlier, deep inside him, roared into hungry, demanding life.

"We should get out of here," he said through gritted teeth.

"I thought you would never ask."

Gabriel took Rosalind's hand and led her from the dance floor, moving swiftly through the crowd and heading straight for the main doors.

"Do you have a coat?" he asked brusquely. At her nod he continued, "Let me get that for you."

She dug in her evening bag and passed him the coat check slip.

"I'll be straight back—don't go anywhere."

He was back in just a moment and helped her shrug into her coat. It seemed like a crime to cover her up but he consoled himself that he would be removing all her layers of clothing before long. He pulled on his own coat and took her by the hand again. Outside, his car was brought to the entrance.

"Your place, or mine?" he asked.

She looked at him for a full ten seconds before answering, giving him a moment to wonder if she had changed her mind.

"How far to your place?" she asked in response. "I'm staying at the Bellamy so if that is closer, I suggest we go there."

"The Bellamy is definitely closer."

He ushered her into his car and closed the door then walked around to the driver's side and settled behind the wheel. It took every ounce of control that he possessed not to spin the car wheels as they left the entrance to the club. While the Bellamy was close, every mile felt like torture. He flicked her a glance from time to time to try to read what she might be thinking, but she kept her gaze firmly forward as his car ate up the distance to the hotel.

Gabe left his car with a parking valet and with his hand on the small of Rosalind's back they stepped inside the hotel lobby. He drew her to a stop as she made a beeline for the elevators.

"Problem?"

He looked deep into her clear, blue eyes searching for any shred of doubt that might be reflected there.

"You're certain about this?" he asked intently.

"Definitely," she answered firmly. "Now let's stop wasting time."

His breath caught in his lungs and he could not have said another word to save himself at that moment. All he could do was follow her to the elevator and then, a few minutes later, down the corridor to her suite. There was no evidence of a tremor in her hand now as she passed her key card over the reader and the green light that glowed on her door handle seemed incredibly symbolic right now.

Rosalind opened the door and stepped into the suite then gestured for him to follow her in. The second he was over the threshold she shoved the door closed, grabbed him by the lapels of his coat, backed him up against the door and kissed him soundly. For a second he was taken aback at the unabashed sensual hunger in her kiss, but that was all it took before he answered in kind.

Her lips were soft and plump and no doubt he was doing a number on the lush red lipstick she'd worn but right now he didn't care. He simply wanted to taste her, all of her, and his hands slipped round to her buttocks and pulled her up hard against him—against the arousal that hadn't fully subsided during their ride to the Bellamy and was now making its own demands.

She tasted of champagne and an underlying sweetness. A flavor he couldn't quite get enough of even as his tongue teased her lips open and allowed him to deepen their kiss. She'd let go of his lapels and was pushing his coat down off his shoulders with short, urgent movements. They broke apart long enough to shed their coats and then she grabbed him again.

"I've been wanting to do this since I met you," she said, before biting softly on his lower lip.

"Just that?" he murmured against her mouth. "There's more of me."

She chuckled and the sound filled him with a combination of joy and desire. This was going to be fun as well as intense. He just knew it. The same way he knew tonight would be like nothing he'd ever done before with anyone else. She was different and with her he could be different, too. He could forget the heartache of his family. He could pretend the distance between him and his father did not exist. And he could relish the fact that while he knew next to nothing about this woman, she knew exactly the same amount of nothing about him, too. They could simply be together. Explore together. Find satisfaction in one another.

Rosalind tugged at his bow tie and her deft fingers made quick work of the knot. She yanked the strip of fabric that he'd so painstakingly tied this evening out from under his collar and cast it to the floor before adroitly flicking the buttons of his shirt open. The second she could pull the fabric away from his chest and bare his skin, she laid her mouth on one of his nipples, nipping gently before pushing his jacket and shirt off and then letting them drop to the floor also.

He wasted no more time. He'd already discerned the whereabouts of the hidden side zipper on her gown while they were dancing and he swiftly drew it down and then slid the garment off her shoulders and down her arms. The fabric slithered down her body, catching slightly on her softly rounded hips. It took the merest push of his hands and the dress joined his clothing that already lay on the floor. His tailor would freak out if he knew, Gabe thought with an ironic twist of his mouth, but then he found his attention magnetically pulled to the stunning vision standing before him.

He groaned as his eyes feasted on her skin. There were no tan lines on her bare breasts, which were exquisitely pert and round. He reached for her, his hands gently cupping her, his thumbs sliding over the taut buds of nipples the color of dark honey. Her pupils enlarged and a glazed look filled the blue depths of her eyes. Her chest flushed with a soft pink.

"I want to taste you." Desire thickened his voice, making it sound like more of a growl. "May I?"

"Oh, yes."

He bent his head and took one nipple between his lips, rolling it with his tongue and drawing the tight bead into his mouth before releasing it again. She trembled against him. Her fingers laced around the back of his head, holding him to her. His hand slid down to her hips, eased beneath the lacy scrap of underwear she wore and eased the fabric down her legs until it, too, dropped to her feet. His hands skimmed the globes of her buttocks, the backs of her shapely thighs. She parted her legs slightly.

"Touch me," she demanded.

He deftly moved one hand around to the front of her leg and then slowly drifted higher. He could feel the heat that emanated from her core and knowing she was hot for him made him desire her all the more. His fingers teased the crease of skin at the apex of her thighs as he brushed backward and forward. She was already wet for him. Her hands had moved to his shoulders and her fingers gripped hold of him so tightly he could feel the impression of her nails against his skin. It was exhilarating and made him feel almost invincible.

He wanted her more than he'd ever wanted anyone before and none of it made sense. They'd only just met and yet here they were. Desperate for one another. His erection was almost painful—he was so hard with the need to bury himself in her body and to feel that heat encase him and grip him hard. He forced himself not to think about it, to solely concentrate on what he was doing to her now. To listen to the sounds of her fractured breathing as he dipped one finger into her honeyed wetness and drew it out again to tease her clit before repeating the movement again.

Her hands were at the belt of his trousers, then

slipping inside the band of his boxer briefs before easing the firm fitting fabric away from him. She took his length in her hand and stroked him from base to tip and back again. He groaned and let his head drop back, allowing sensation to ripple through him.

"I want you inside me," she ground out.

"Believe me, I want that, too," he growled back.

"Now, please!"

She lifted one leg over his hip and he shifted his hands to her buttocks, eased her higher until he could feel his tip at the heated entrance to her body.

"Gabe, now!"

"Protection," he muttered, straining to hold himself back even while his body urged him to simply take her as she'd insisted.

"I'm safe. I'm on the pill—I have a clean bill of health. Please, Gabe, don't leave me hanging."

He knew he was clean; testing had been a pre-entry requirement with the marriage broker, and could wait no longer. Pushing her hard against the wall he entered her body in a single stroke.

"Yessss," she hissed against his ear.

It was madness and perfection all at once; he realized as his hips moved in the age-old rhythm of time, harder and faster until he felt himself on the edge of climax. But he wouldn't let go, couldn't. Not until she found her satisfaction. He opened his eyes and looked at her. Rosalind's cheeks were flushed, her eyes glittering with arousal, her lips parted on rapid breaths. A long slow moan ripped from her body and he felt her inner muscles clench around him, then tighter again as her orgasm poured through her. It felt as if she'd given him an incredible gift, this intimacy of watching her come and it was enough to send him over the edge as the waves of his own pleasure burst from behind the stop bank of his self-control and swamped him.

He wasn't sure how long they stayed like that. Their breathing hard and fast, their bodies slick with perspiration. Their legs trembling with the force of their joint release. Eventually though, she let her leg slide back down again and he reluctantly pulled free of her body.

"You okay?" he asked. Things had gotten quite tempestuous there.

She smiled at him like a cat that got the cream. "Oh, yeah. That was great, for a starter."

His lips quirked back in response. "Starter?"

"Well, there's still the main and dessert to follow, right?"

His grin widened. "Right."

He stepped from his pants and discarded his shoes and socks and watched as she walked across the suite to the bedroom. The sight of her, naked except for the sinfully sexy high heels she wore, was enough to bring him rapidly back to aching life again. He followed her into the bedroom and onto the bed.

Far from what he'd been expecting when he'd left

the house to go to the club this evening, tonight was turning into a very good night indeed.

Gabe reluctantly let himself out of Rosalind's suite a few hours later. It had been tempting to stay and linger longer but he needed to get home to the ranch, get showered and dressed and return to town in time for his breakfast meeting at the Royal Diner.

All through his drive home he replayed the night he'd had with the exquisite and talented Ms. Rosalind Banks. They'd connected so intimately in the bedroom—and out of it too, he remembered with a broad grin. And even though he hadn't snatched more than an hour or two of sleep, he felt invigorated in a way he hadn't felt in a very long time. It was probably just as well they weren't suited as far as his Grand Plan for his future went. He already felt the kind of emotional pull to return to her that he'd sworn he wouldn't allow himself to feel again for any woman.

No, Rosalind Banks was good for one night—better than good—and that's where it began and ended. For them both. Their individual expectations were not compatible with what they each wanted out of life—a shame, really, but it couldn't be helped.

He turned his mind to the potential wife candidate he was meeting this morning. The matchmaker had only provided a photo and the basics of height, weight and employment, but nothing personal. Nothing like how she'd smell when he got close and lifted her hair to nuzzle her neck. Nothing like how soft her skin would feel beneath his lightly calloused fingers.

Gabe dragged his thoughts back to the road ahead of him. Nope, he wasn't going there. That way led straight to the woman he'd left in tangled sheets and a warm bed. By the time he'd reached the ranch, rushed through his ablutions, re-dressed and headed back out to the diner, weariness started to pull at him. Maybe this wasn't such a great idea, but it was too late to back out now. He'd paid his fee; he'd made his expectations explicitly clear and the matchmaker had promised to deliver.

And deliver she did. The prospective wife candidate was a beautiful, poised and accomplished woman. In fact, in many ways she was a feminine version of himself. Jaded by love but still hoping for stability and family. But no matter how perfectly they were suited—and if you'd asked him yesterday, he would have said she was hands-down exactly what he was looking for—he couldn't summon even a speck of interest. He'd at least hoped that his prospective bride would light some spark within him.

He pushed a piece of bacon onto his fork and swirled it around in the maple syrup that had poured off his pancake stack and wondered what Rosalind was eating for breakfast, before snapping his attention back to his date.

"I'm sorry, what was that you said?" he enquired, trying to inject something in his voice that would say he was anything but bored out of his mind.

"That woman over there, she keeps staring at you. And look, now she's coming over to our table."

Gabe looked up in time to see a petite, blond woman stride confidently toward their table.

"Friend of yours?" his date asked.

"No friend of mine."

He recognized her immediately. Sierra Morgan. The reporter for *America* magazine. She also free-lanced for the Royal Gazette, recently doing a story about Cammie Wentworth finding a baby boy in his capsule, left on the trunk of her car. Ms. Morgan originally came to Royal to do a story on the tenth anniversary of the Texas Cattleman's Club finally admitting women, but she kept ferreting around for another story and had pestered him about his family history before. He'd put her off but now he had the distinct feeling she wasn't going to be put off a moment longer.

"Hi," she said with a wide grin as she reached the table. "Mr. Carrington, you remember me, don't you? Sierra Morgan, investigative journalist."

"A reporter?" Gabe's wife candidate stared at him in irritation. "I'm not talking to any reporter. My private life is exactly that. And, to be honest, I don't think you're what I'm looking for. Thank you for breakfast, but I'm out."

And with that, she rose to her feet, grabbed her bag and headed for the door. Gabe watched in stunned amazement.

"Was it something I said?" Sierra Morgan asked as she eased into the recently vacated seat.

Gabe turned his gaze on her. "Looks like it."

"I'm sorry, but I really wanted to catch you. You know I want to interview you about your family history and now's as good a time as any, right?"

Actually, no time was a good time as far as he was concerned.

"My family history is not up for discussion," he said firmly and pushed his plate aside, all appetite now gone.

"Look, let me at least run something by you. See if it rings any bells in the family-skeleton department."

She was nothing if not persistent. Gabe sighed and raised a hand to order more coffee.

"Fine," he said. Maybe the quickest way to get rid of her for good was to hear her out. "I'll listen, but that's it."

She smiled her thanks and added her coffee order when the waitress came over. When the coffee arrived, she took a gulp then put the mug down on the table in front of her, her hands cupping the ceramic, and leaning her elbows on the table.

"You know that baby Micah's mom, Arielle Martin, had been working at the Royal Assisted Living Center before she died, right? I understand you met her?"

Gabe nodded. He'd heard about the poor woman's passing and knew from their brief meeting that she'd been a budding photojournalist before her tragic death. Was that where Sierra was coming from? Did they have some professional link?

"Her diary tells us that she was fascinated by the centenarian who lives there, Harmon Wentworth. He told her a story that his powerful family had kept hush-hush, but that now he's decided that maybe it's time for someone to find out the truth. You know he discovered late in life that he was adopted by the Wentworth family. Well, it turns out that Arielle had some notes in her diary that suggest that Harmon is possibly connected to the Langley family."

Gabe felt a prick of concern. The Langley family members were long-standing Royal inhabitants, in fact they dated right back to the founding of the Texas Cattleman's Club many years ago. He knew Sierra was in town to write about the special anniversary of the club, but what the hell else had she unearthed?

"Carry on," he encouraged.

"Well, from what I can tell, Arielle tried to talk to the Wentworths about the link, but they clammed up, politely but very definitely telling her they would not discuss the matter. But she kept digging and she's mentioned another name in her diary, Violetta Ford, underlined three times, so it obviously was important to her."

Gabe had heard about the Ford woman. She'd been considered a rebel in her day, a confirmed spinster who'd run her own small ranch single-handedly until being joined by a young cowgirl, Emmalou Hilliard, who was now ninety-nine years old. As a rancher, Violetta Ford had demanded to be admitted to the newly founded Texas Cattleman's Club, but her gender had made her ineligible. Something she hadn't accepted well it seemed, because she'd sold up and left town permanently not long after her request for membership had been emphatically denied.

Sierra was still talking so he turned his mind back to what she was saying.

"I think this Violetta Ford could have been Harmon Wentworth's birth mother but I need to find someone who might have heard an old family story about her possibly having an affair with another rancher in the district. I know your family were neighbors of the Wentworths back then and I know from Arielle's diary that she spoke to you about your family history. Can you shed any more light on this for me? Have you heard of Violetta Ford and could one of your ancestors possibly have had an affair with her?"

Gabe slowly shook his head. This was getting so convoluted even he, who had a mind like a steel trap, was getting muddled.

"Everyone here has heard of Violetta Ford but you're barking up the wrong tree if you think she was Harmon Wentworth's birth mother. You can barely keep a secret in Royal these days—can you imagine how much more difficult it would have been back then with its much smaller population? Ms. Morgan, you really need to try again to talk to the Wentworths about this. I certainly can't help you and I know for sure that no one in my family would be interested in digging up old stories."

The journalist huffed a sharp breath in frustration. "What is it with you people? Aren't you interested in helping out an old man to find his true roots? Is no one here interested in the past?"

"You'll find we're passionate about protecting the past and our people. I'm sorry, but that's all I'm prepared to say."

"Fine, well, you haven't seen the last of me. I'm not giving up."

He watched her gather her things and leave. For a small woman she moved with huge energy. His coffee had gone cold so he flicked several bills on the table and got up to head back to the ranch. Outside, he saw the indubitable Ms. Morgan get behind the wheel of her car and drive away. She was nothing if not persistent. Trouble was, what the hell was she going to unearth with that strength of determination?

Three

December

Rosalind knew she'd been eating the right things and getting enough rest; goodness knew she needed naps and more sleep at night than she ever had before. She'd put it down to the frenetic workload she'd given herself once she hit New York, starting with finding accommodation that she could work out of in the short term, and continuing with meetings with buyers for various retail groups and smaller exclusive boutique owners who could feature her ranges.

They were running at a massive loss on the leisurewear range, but Piers was optimistic that the pop-up stores through Australia and New Zealand during this whole month of December would be a huge hit. She could only keep her fingers crossed that he was right and hope that the new designs she'd worked up and costed would appeal to the new players she was targeting here in America.

All this travel and time zone changes and the demands of her work had really taken a toll, she thought as she dressed in one of her leisure-wear outfits and went to her automatic coffee maker which had her favorite brew ready and waiting, its aroma filling the tiny kitchen the way it did every morning. She took one step into the kitchen, however, and did an abrupt about-face and headed straight to the bathroom as a huge wave of nausea hit her. She managed not to throw up and the cold facecloth she bathed her face and the back of her neck with was a huge help, but when she looked at herself in the mirror, she knew she couldn't deny it any longer.

There was a distinct possibility she was pregnant. Admitting the news to herself wasn't quite as shocking as she'd anticipated. She'd always wanted kids, but she'd also always hoped for the love and marriage part, first. Having a baby now was the worst possible timing, especially here in New York on her own with no physical support network to help her out. And with her business holding on by a thread she had two choices—buy into Gabriel Carrington's marriage of convenience, if he was still available, or go home. To calm her mind, she started to make a list; at the top was buying a home pregnancy test and finding out if she was, indeed, pregnant. Then, if she was pregnant, she had to let Gabriel Carrington know he was going to be a daddy.

It shocked her to realize he'd never been far from her thoughts this past month, even more so than her disappointment that Drake had so clearly moved on without her. In fact, she'd barely spared Drake a thought. Shouldn't she have been more cut up about him? While they'd only been together a little under six months, she'd been prepared to spend her life with him and now it looked as though she'd have a lifelong contact with one of his peers instead. And for some crazy mixed-up reason, that knowledge sent a thrill of anticipation through her.

She and Gabe had experienced such a powerful connection, but could they build on that? She only hoped. What if he had already found his perfect wife candidate and entered into a contract? The thought pinged an emotion not unlike envy, which surprised her and made her reexamine her feelings for Gabriel in a new light. Ros had thought she'd been thinking solely in terms of the baby but it wasn't just about a child anymore, was it? She really wanted to see Gabe again, get to know him better, maybe even fall in love even if he said he didn't believe in such a thing—after all, they'd been bloody amazing in bed; surely they could find common ground in other areas, too.

From what he'd said at the gala, he'd expect her to marry him and she wasn't sure how she felt about that. She'd always considered marriage the penultimate goal of a strong and loving relationship, with a family coming next to seal everything. They barely knew one another, but they were going to be parents together. He wasn't looking for love and she knew she couldn't live with a loveless future. So where did that leave them? She had no doubt that with mutual respect they could make a marriage work, but would that be enough for her? She had to hope so or this entire situation became impossible, no matter which way she turned it. Ros snorted and looked at herself in the mirror. Here she was overthinking things when she didn't even know for sure if she was pregnant. One hand settled on her lower belly and she continued to look at her reflection. Pregnant. It felt oddly right thinking about bringing a child into her life even if the timing was all wrong. But a child shared with a man who didn't believe in love? It could make for a rocky future.

She tipped out the coffee carafe and made a cup of tea and some toast. While she ate and sipped her tea, she added to her list. One, find out if she was expecting. Everything hinged on that result. Then when she knew, it would either be life as normal, or she'd be searching flights to Royal.

At the drugstore she bought three tests, just to be certain. Twenty minutes later she had her answer. Positive. Positive. Positive. She was having a baby. The truth of it was exhilarating and terrifying in equal proportion. She hugged the news to herself for the rest of the day while she decided how best to approach Gabe. A phone call wouldn't cut it; she knew that. She had to tell him face-to-face.

Before Rosalind could change her mind, she looked up flights online and made her booking. That done, she reached deep into her wardrobe, hauled out her suitcase and began to throw things into it. She had no idea what she needed or how long she'd be there. That it would be cold was a given, but hopefully not as cold as New York. Her furnished apartment was paid up until the end of December and by then she'd know for certain if she was returning to it, or not. She tossed in her sketchbooks and art supplies while she was at it. No one said she'd have to stop working while she was there.

Three hours later she was on her way to the airport, that weird feeling in her belly one of nerves rather than nausea. How would he take the news and what if he'd already found that wife he was looking for? She just had to wait and find out.

Gabe looked up from his office desk as a chime warned him of a vehicle coming up the long driveway to his home. He didn't recognize the midsize SUV that travelled slowly as if the driver was unfamiliar with both the vehicle and the terrain. He rose from his desk and walked to the window and watched as the SUV pulled up outside his house and the driver's door flung open. Every muscle in his body pulled tight as he identified the curvy blonde figure that alighted.

Rosalind Banks. The last woman he expected to see either here or anywhere else, for that matter. He took the opportunity to study her carefully. It had been a month since he'd left her at the Bellamy. A month where he'd interviewed and rejected several potential candidates for what he now called Project Wife. And it was all her fault. For some idiotic reason, he hadn't been able to get her out of his mind and, equally stupidly, he'd held every other woman up to her image and found them wanting.

He thought he'd seen the last of her, so what the hell was she doing here and how had she found where he lived? She looked tired, paler than he remembered and the jeans she wore with a totally impractical pair of heeled ankle boots looked as if they'd been painted on her long legs. Something inside him hitched hard as he remembered those legs wrapped around his waist as he entered her body. He forced the memory from his mind. That was half his problem these days. Not being able to keep those sneaky thoughts of her from interrupting him at the most inconvenient moments. Hell, they'd barely known one another and yet she'd snuck under his skin like a burr under a saddle.

As he watched, she seemed to pull herself up a little taller and square her shoulders before making her way up the shallow stairs that led to the entrance to his single-story sprawling home settled atop a small hill. Gabe turned from the window and headed toward the entrance hall.

Rosalind looked a little taken aback as he opened the door.

"Oh, hi, I wasn't sure you'd be home, or out there somewhere." She gestured toward the range that spread as far as the eye could see.

"As you can see, I'm home. I didn't expect to see you again. How did you know where to find me?"

"I asked at a gas station just out of town. But..." She hesitated and chewed on that deliciously full lower lip for a moment before sucking in a deep breath and continuing. "Something came up. Something I needed to discuss with you, urgently."

"You'd better come in then. Follow me."

He closed the door behind her and led her to the inviting family room near his kitchen. The couches here were long and comfortable and bracketed the double-sided fireplace that also opened onto a casual dining area on the other side. The tall brick chimney that stretched to the top of the double-height ceiling featured a wagon wheel from his great-grandfather's first wagon. Gabriel liked the reminder of where and who his family had sprung from and the permanence of the Carrington family on the landscape here. One day this would all belong to his heir—provided he reached a satisfying conclusion to Project Wife.

"Take a seat. Can I get you anything to drink? A coffee, water, something stronger?"

"Water would be great, thank you."

He nodded and went to the kitchen where he grabbed a couple of water bottles and glasses. He brought them through, pouring Rosalind's out for her and handing her the glass. The moment their fingers brushed he was aware of that sizzling reaction he'd experienced the first time he'd touched her. Seems time had not allowed that primal reaction to abate at all. Obviously one torrid night with Ms. Banks had not been enough, but he wasn't into a short-term fling, he reminded himself. He was on the hunt for a wife and he and Rosalind were on different trajectories when it came to that no matter how compatible they'd been in the bedroom.

"What brings you back to Royal?" he asked, settling on the couch opposite hers. "You mentioned needing to discuss something with me urgently?"

For all she'd used the word *urgent* she didn't appear to be in a hurry to fill him in on the reason behind her unexpected visit. Instead, she gave him a weak smile and took a long gulp of her water. She set her glass down on the coaster on the table in front of her and hitched forward a little on her seat, her fingers clasped tightly on her knees. He didn't know her well but he was pretty good at reading people and she clearly didn't expect him to take whatever it was that she was here to tell him very well.

"Yes, a…complication relating to our night together," she said softly, her eyes dropping to the thick rug on the floor at her booted feet.

"A complication?"

Gabe pushed back the burr of irritation that made him want to urge her to just get on with what she'd come to say. He waited, his eyes fixed on the top of her head. When she looked up, their eyes locked and he saw the muscles in her throat work nervously as she swallowed.

"I'm pregnant," she said.

A roaring sound filled his ears and he shook his head slightly. "You're what?"

"Pregnant. With your baby."

"Are you sure?"

"That I'm pregnant or that it's yours?" she said with a slight bite to her tone.

"Yeah." For all he knew, she could have been with any number of men before or after that night they spent together.

"I am. To both. I must have made a mistake with my pill with the time zone changes and everything but I can assure you that the baby is definitely yours."

Her voice was clipped and she reached for her glass again. This time her hand shook a little as she tipped the liquid into her mouth.

"Well," Gabe said and then ran out of steam as to what to say next. A baby? *His* baby? Wasn't that what he wanted all along?

"Yeah, *well*," she repeated. "Obviously this is very inconvenient for both of us. I only just found out and I didn't think it was the kind of thing I could tell you on the phone, even if I had your number. But I wanted you to know before..."

"Before?" Gabe's blood ran cold. Instinct surged and the need to protect and provide for his child bloomed from deep inside.

She shrugged. "I don't know. Before I made my mind up about what I should do, I guess. To be honest, I didn't think much past telling you. Look, we got on pretty well that night we met and I think we could make this work. But if you're not interested, or if you're already married, then I'll go back to Australia. I can't bring this child up on my own."

Got on pretty well? The woman was a master of understatement. Even now, looking at her, all he wanted to do was take her in his arms and give in to the desire to kiss and taste every part of her body. But then the second part of what she said sank in. Head back to Australia? No way. If she did that he'd likely never see his child again—or her, a tiny voice tickled at the back of his mind. Ice ran in his veins.

"No," he said bluntly.

"No, what?"

"No, you're not taking this baby, if it is my baby, to Australia. He or she will stay here and be raised as a Carrington."

"It is your baby, Gabriel," she said softly. "I swear."

He looked deep into her blue eyes and saw the honesty that reflected back at him and knew, deep in his gut, she wasn't lying about this.

"We'll get married," he said firmly.

"I figured you'd say that. Are you sure that's the

best thing to do? We don't even know each other. You're prepared to marry a complete stranger?"

"Not a *complete* stranger," he answered and watched as she blushed at his words.

"You know what I mean," she snapped. "This isn't a joking matter, Gabe."

"No, it isn't, and I am serious. Marry me. You'll be free to pursue your business interests and I will have the heir I wanted."

Her mouth twisted ruefully. "And what about us? As a couple? Will we be…intimate?"

He felt a thrill of excitement at the thought and quelled it rapidly. That wasn't what he wanted. He'd seen what unrealistic expectations of love did to people. If he could keep this clinical, no one would get hurt. "I wouldn't want it to lead to any misunderstandings or complications," he hedged.

"Complications like falling in love?" she asked bluntly.

"Exactly."

Ros fell silent and chewed on her lower lip again. He found his gaze fixated on that part of her, remembering the feel and the texture of her lips, her whole mouth, beneath his and on his body. Heat flared deep inside him and the urge to relive the night they'd spent together flared along with it.

He sounded so adamant—his single-word response reverberating through her. Love, to him, was a problem, not a joyful sharing of life and emotions and happiness. She didn't know how she'd cope without that. She flicked her eyes to where he sat opposite her, patiently waiting for her response. Or not quite so patiently, she realized, as she noted the vein pulsing rapidly on the side of his neck. Perhaps he wasn't quite so calm about this after all.

And nor was she. Seeing him again had reminded her of how beautifully they'd meshed and melded together that night. The passion between them had been off the scale. Even now, just looking at him, in casual jeans and a fitted black sweater that clung to every line of his torso like a lover's caress, made her heart rate pick up and her breasts feel full and heavy, longing for the touch of his incredibly talented long fingers. Of the touch of his lips and tongue.

Rosalind squirmed slightly on the couch but it offered her no relief from the discomfort that her arousal brought. There was only one thing that would assuage that, she thought ruefully.

Could she do it? Could she accept his crazy proposal? And what if they never made love—ever—because it, in his words, could make things complicated? This entire situation made no sense to her at all. She'd always wanted love and marriage and a family—in that order. Was it ridiculous of her to want what her parents and so many of her friends had? But the fact remained everything was happening in reverse. She was carrying Gabe's baby and she owed this little stranger inside her body the very best of everything and that included their father being a very present person in their life. There was no doubt that Gabe fully expected to be that person and that he could offer the best of everything to his son or daughter, especially if this home was anything to go by. And what of love? She didn't doubt that Gabe would love their baby with every fiber of his being. It was clear in the determined and implacable way he'd presented her with his solution to her current predicament. But could she live her life without at least the expectation of love? Would financial security be enough?

If she said no, she'd have to return to Sydney and try to pick up the pieces of her business there, which would diminish her chances of successfully breaking into the market here in the States and inevitably lead to staff losses and a massive drop in brand awareness—not to mention the complications of megalong-distance shared custody. If she said yes, she'd receive a cash injection to her business that would allow her to keep her employees on and to make an aggressive push to expand right alongside being an active daily part of her baby's life.

One thing was certain. There was no chance to potentially develop a relationship with her baby's father if she moved back home, and she wanted that opportunity. Accepting that truth left her with only one answer.

"Yes," she said.

Four

Gabe looked around him at the small group of guests he'd invited to celebrate his and Rosalind's nuptials here at the Club. Given the short notice, not everyone he'd invited had been able to attend but of those who could, it was great to see the lack of judgment as they'd been introduced to his new bride.

He rolled the word around in his mind a moment or two. He still couldn't believe they'd pulled this together in a little under five days but from the moment she'd said yes to him, he'd put things in motion with his lawyer and managed to find a local doctor who could care for Rosalind during her pregnancy. One of his dad's cronies, a judge, had been only too happy to marry them in his chambers after the requisite seventy-two hour wait time from when their application to marry had been approved.

Gabe's father, as usual, had been unavailable and his grandfather was out of town. He'd only invited them as a matter of courtesy and had been relieved when Denver Carrington had sent his apologies, with an invitation to lunch at a later date. Gabe had accepted the invitation, happy to end the call to his dad as quickly as possible. He watched as Rosalind laughed at something one of his friends said and wondered what his mother would think of the whole situation. She had loved her husband dearly and he'd stomped all over that love with steel-capped boots. Would she be sorry that her only son had chosen a practical marriage versus one that might risk his heart?

He took a sip of the very fine champagne being circulated freely around the room and turned as one of their guests hailed him.

"Gabe, congratulations."

Carson Wentworth approached him with a genuine smile wreathing his face. The current president of the Texas Cattleman's Club, Carson had beaten the next-strongest candidate, Lana Langley, by a decent margin but his win had only served to feed the flames of the ongoing feud between the two families.

"I see you got your wish," Carson said as he stopped next to Gabe.

"Thanks, Carson. Glad you could make it to celebrate with us."

"To be honest, I thought you had a pretty tall order when I heard the rumors about you looking for a wife. I understood marriages of convenience went out with the horse and cart." Carson laughed and raised his glass in a toast. "But I mean it when I say congratulations. I met Rosalind just now and she's a keeper. Intelligent and beautiful. You two make a perfect pair. I hope you grow to be very happy together."

Gabe raised his glass in acknowledgment and took another sip. It seemed that Rosalind was winning everyone over. Even himself, which was something he neither anticipated nor truly wanted. He had no difficulty with liking her but, annoyingly, he found himself thinking about her all the time, even looking forward to seeing her when they'd met for their various appointments and wedding planning in the days preceding their ceremony.

"We suit one another and we're both committed to making this work," he said firmly. "Say, how's your great-grandfather doing? It's been a while since I've seen him."

Carson frowned. "He's doing okay. Frailer now, of course, but that's only to be expected given he's a hundred years old. If anything, though, his mind is even sharper than before, with the exception of this bee he has in his bonnet about being adopted. If it is true, I can understand why he wants to find closure before he passes away, but the chances of finding out anything new at this stage are pretty slim."

"I keep hearing about this diary of that photojournalist, Arielle Martin. Do you think she uncovered anything important before she died?"

"There are rumors and apparently he told her something in confidence, but you know as well as I do that all too often rumors are not based in fact, especially around here. Oh, and that's not all Harmon is obsessed with. He's been harping on about ending the feud between the Langleys and the Wentworths. Says it's gone on long enough. From my side of the fence, I'm more than happy to lay down arms, so to speak, but I doubt the Langleys are as keen. Especially since I beat Lana to the presidency here at the club. Trouble is, Harmon has made it clear that if there isn't some kind of truce soon, he's going to take the club out of his will."

Carson looked deeply concerned by this new revelation.

"The club's solvent enough without his bequest, surely?" Gabe asked.

"Yes, but we want to do bigger and better things for the entire community of Royal. That's going to take big money, too."

Before he could discuss the problem any further, they were interrupted by Rosalind. Gabe let his eyes roam over her, hardly daring to believe this enticing creature was not only his wife, but also carrying his child. It punched something deep inside him, making him feel a connection to her that he was ill equipped to handle right now. He hadn't expected to feel like that. Hadn't wanted to. And yet, she'd somehow begun to slip beneath his defenses and nestle somewhere within the fortress of his heart. He cast the idea aside as quickly as it bloomed in his mind. His heart was not engaged in this venture. That was not what this was about.

Even so, he'd barely been able to tear his eyes from Rosalind. Dressed in an ivory knee-length dress which had a floor-length overskirt of something light and filmy that caught the light and glittered softly as she moved and with her hair flowing loose over her shoulders, she had an almost ethereal look. And she was his. That knowledge fed something in him he didn't even know he craved. Craving was not part of their contract, he reminded himself firmly. For now, it was enough that she'd agreed to his terms and that he'd agreed to hers. Their marriage was an amicable legal agreement and he needed to remind himself to keep it that way.

"They're going to start the dancing soon," she said, putting a hand on his arm and leaning up to talk to him more privately. "Are you up for it?"

They'd discussed this earlier but hadn't reached a decision. They'd had to pull everything together so quickly that thinking about a wedding dance had been the last thing on his mind. But now that the ink was dry on their marriage maybe it was time to relax and actually enjoy the evening.

"Always," he said, taking her hand in his and giving it a light squeeze. “Carson, would you excuse us? We have a dance to enjoy together.”

“By all means,” Carson said with a broad grin. “Don’t let me stop you.”

Gabe led Rosalind toward the dance floor of the function room and nodded toward the leader of the band the club had hired. The man nodded back and drew the set they’d been playing to a halt. Then, with an announcement to the crowd to welcome the newly wed Mr. and Mrs. Carrington to the floor, the band swung into a slow dance. Gabe pulled Ros into his arms and guided her around the floor. Around the perimeter, many of his friends applauded vigorously before, two by two, joining them. He knew no one had expected him to pull this off, in fact, many had counselled him against such a partnership, but a sense of exhilaration filled him as he and Ros danced smoothly together and he realized that his goal had been unequivocally achieved.

“You look pleased with yourself,” Ros said, looking up at him with a smile.

“I am.”

“It’s all gone well today, hasn’t it?” she said with a note of satisfaction. “And everyone has been quite welcoming. I didn’t really expect such a turnout. Do you think they’re all here because they’re curious about me or because they wanted to take advantage of your generosity in throwing a big party?”

“Maybe they’re just happy for us,” Gabe said, but

he couldn't deny that she was likely correct about their curiosity about her.

"We both know that is a big reach of the imagination."

"Well, there are always romantics in every situation. People who view the world through rose-tinted glasses and are always looking for the happy-ever-after."

"People like me, you mean?" she asked pointedly.

"But even you saw the practicality of our arrangement," he responded.

"I didn't really have a lot of choice, but yes. Our arrangement is practical, for both of us. By the way, thank you for the advance of funds. My operations manager confirmed receipt of it today. It will go a long way toward providing stability for my team."

"I'm glad it is going to good use. To be honest, when I first came up with the idea of this marriage arrangement, I expected whoever I ended up with would likely be more frivolous with the settlement. But you're not like that, are you?"

"We really don't know each other at all, do we?" she said, a note of concern in her voice. "This is going to work, isn't it?"

"Of course it is. We know exactly where we both stand. There are no messy feelings involved nor unreasonable expectations from either of us of one another. Most importantly, our child will be loved and provided for more than amply. What could go wrong?"

"Shh, don't tempt fate," she said. "Look, we both know what we entered this marriage for. Neither of us are children. It wasn't what I expected for my future but I'm going to give it my very best to ensure I hold up my end of the deal."

"Then we remain in agreement. See, it's not so hard. We've got this marriage thing down." He laughed a little but could sense she still suffered some concern about their situation.

She huffed out a short breath before replying. "We've been married for all of five hours. We can hardly use this as an example of how things will continue between us."

"But you forget, in the past few days we've spent many, many hours together working out the important things that most couples don't or won't face up to until it's all falling apart. We have everything bound up neatly and put in place to ensure our marital stability."

"Yes, we do," she agreed. "I'm a little tired—do you mind if we sit the next one out?"

"Of course we can. We can even slip away soon, if you'd prefer to head home."

Home. He meant his home, of course. She had no idea if or when the sprawling ranch house built of wood and stone where he lived would ever feel like home to her. It was so different from everything she'd ever known. The wide, open spaces that surrounded the house, the stock, the horses—it was a foreign land to this city girl and she felt thoroughly displaced.

To hold on to the last remnants of normalcy in her life, she'd remained at the Bellamy since her return to Royal. From there she'd arranged for the last of her personal items to be shipped from her New York apartment but she hadn't quite been able to bring herself to cancel the lease just yet. Realistically, she knew she didn't need to keep the place but a small part of her wanted to ensure she had somewhere to escape to, should she need it. A place that was still hers outside the life she'd been absorbed into here in Royal.

Wow, and as if that didn't sound dramatic, she castigated herself silently as Gabe led her to a quieter seating area just off the main function room. Before they could leave, however, a young woman with fine blond hair and a slight build walked up to them, a camera slung around her neck and a notebook and pen in her hands.

"Congratulations," she said with a big smile. "Would you mind posing for a photo for the local paper? I'd love to do a small feature on the two of you, if you have a moment."

"Ms. Morgan, this is a private function. Invited guests only. What are you doing here?" Gabe said in a forbidding tone.

The woman continued to smile but Ros noted that her green eyes didn't quite reflect the friendliness she was projecting.

"Mr. Carrington, you know I'm doing some freelancing since I'm in town. This is a bit of fluff for the local paper, not an attack on your family's integrity or asking you to haul any skeletons from the closet," she said patiently. "Please, just a photo, then."

"Gabe," Ros said softly to her husband. "We can do a photo, surely."

His arm was rigid beneath her hand but he turned to her and asked, "Are you sure?"

"Of course. Better that our marriage is publicized on our terms than as the subject of gossip, right?"

He took a moment to consider her words before nodding to the reporter who'd avidly watched the interplay between them.

"Fine, a photo."

"Great, thank you. If you two could stand a little closer…closer still. Yes, like that."

She continued to fire directions at them as she took several shots. Ros had curved her arm around Gabe's back, under his jacket, and the heat from his body suffused her arm and spread slowly through her body. He still held himself quite rigid, as though this entire thing was a torment. And maybe to him it was. She herself was used to being around cameras but not often the subject of them. By the time the reporter stopped taking pictures Ros was done with smiling and posing. It gave her a new appreciation for her models, who went through this every day of their working lives.

"These are great! Thank you both," she exclaimed brightly.

The woman turned and strode away, tucking her notebook and pen in her large bag as she did.

"There, that was relatively painless," Ros said with a smile at Gabe.

"For you, maybe. I prefer to keep my private life, private."

He led her to a smaller seating area away from their function room. The chairs were deep and comfortable and the room was uninhabited except for a staff member cleaning glasses at the bar off to one side.

"I'll get you some water," he said after she'd settled in a chair.

"A cup of tea would be nice. Hot tea, with a dash of milk. English Breakfast if they have it."

"In a land of sweetened cold tea drinkers that might be a stretch but I'm sure I'll be able to rustle up something for you," he said with a teasing smile.

That smile sent a bolt of awareness deep into her core. The man was almost unlawfully good looking. And he was her husband! She looked down at the ornate diamond wedding ring he'd placed on her finger in the judge's chambers earlier today. It was a beautiful piece of jewelry but it felt heavy and foreign on her finger. His own ring had been far simpler and her fingers had trembled as she'd slid the heavy gold signet ring embedded with a single diamond and engraved with his initials onto his finger.

The importance of what she'd agreed to do had been underlined by the simple act of exchanging rings. The relief she'd experienced in that moment had been palpable. And, of course, it wasn't just knowing her staff would be okay, but the baby she was carrying, too. She had a responsibility to ensure her baby had the best life she could provide, something she was increasingly anxious about. After all, what did she know about raising a child?

Gabe was trying so hard to make everything feel normal, or as normal as it got when you'd just hitched yourself to a virtual stranger. But he hadn't forced her into this marriage, she reminded herself. She'd gone into this with her eyes wide open and her business would survive as a result of it. And their baby would want for nothing. Nor would she, financially at least. Gabe had been more than generous with the marriage settlement which had been designed to buoy her business through this difficult time.

But emotionally? Would she be able to live her life without the tenets of a long and happy marriage—love, commitment to one another, like minds—the way her parents had?

Gabe returned with a small tray.

"Just regular black tea, I'm afraid. But piping hot with not a touch of sweetener to be seen or tasted," he said, setting the tray down on the side table by her chair.

"Thank you. I'm sure it'll revive me in a minute or two."

"Seriously, I meant it when I said we could head home if you'd prefer. No one will blame us. It is our wedding night after all."

But would it be a normal wedding night? Ros wondered on an unexpected surge of desire that chased away her weariness and replaced it with a thrum of something far more primal. She made a decision.

"Okay, let me have a cup of this tea and after that we'll go."

"Good, I'll have my car brought round. Take your time over the tea."

He was gone again leaving her to watch his tall figure striding purposefully away. Even watching him from the back made everything ping in her body. There was latent strength in the way he moved, purpose in every step. He was utterly mesmerizing. Once he was out of sight, she poured the tea, added a dash of milk and lifted the cup to take a sip. She sighed with pleasure. The tea was perfect and just what she felt like right now. She was grateful for his consideration in getting it for her.

But that gratitude didn't stop a quiver of unease from rippling through her as she wondered anew how this would all work out. On paper everything had made sense, but her emotions were beginning to spiral on different tangents right now. She was fiercely attracted to him on a physical level and she knew that if they could enjoy intimacy together they stood a very good chance of making their marriage work, of developing strong feelings for one another. She wanted that to the depths of her soul and the optimist that dwelled inside her hoped they could achieve it. But could she crack the fierce control he had on his emotions? Could she get him to open up to her and let her into his heart the way she was willing to let him into hers?

As if she'd willingly conjured him up, Gabe reappeared striding back toward her and she felt a flutter of awareness as he approached.

"How's the tea?" he asked, sitting next to her and draping one arm across the back of her shoulders.

His fingers lightly brushed the top of her arm through the gossamer-fine overcoat she wore with her dress, making every nerve in her body focus on the sensations he created with his casual touch.

"Perfect. I'm feeling a lot better already. Seriously, if you want to stay longer, I'll manage."

"No, I'm all good to head home. I've already let a couple of people know we're slipping away."

Ros put her cup and saucer down and gave him a smile. "Shall we go, then?"

In answer, Gabe rose to his feet again and held out a hand to help her up. Their eyes met and there was that smile again, the one that made the corners of his eyes crinkle just a bit and made the almost obsidian darkness of his irises gleam. Again, she felt that tug of longing. She'd heard that pregnancy could make a woman more sexually responsive—was that what was happening here or was it simply his magnetism that had her all tied up in knots?

A club staff member brought Ros's wrap and bag for her as they passed through the lobby. Through the main doors she could see Gabe's car gleaming outside. This was to be her life from now on, she reminded herself. She was used to wealth and privilege, after all she'd grown up as a child of a diplomat, but the rarified air of the club together with the obvious wealth so casually displayed by so many of its members was next-level. Life was getting very interesting, indeed.

Five

Ros hadn't paid all that much mind to the distance between Royal and Gabe's ranch when she'd arrived in town the other day but the forty-minute drive there now gave her some idea of the distance involved. Especially when the only lights she saw, aside from the roadside lighting, were from well-spaced ranch houses well into the distance.

"Doesn't the isolation bother you?" she asked, breaking the silence that had lasted between them since they'd pulled away from the club.

"Isolation? Nah, I never think of it that way. I have a ranch manager, Pete, and his wife, Doreen, who is my housekeeper, and their family that live on site as well as Cookie and my ranch hands, some of whom have wives and kids, too. We're our own small community within my own boundaries. I like that no one else can tell me what to do there."

She weighed his words and considered her reply carefully before speaking. "You don't like being told what to do?"

"Does anyone?" He laughed and spared her a glance before focusing on the road ahead. "You're your own boss. I bet you don't like being told what to do, either."

"You're right, I don't. It's one of the reasons I like to surround myself with 'yes' men," she teased. "But you're not a 'yes' man, are you?"

She turned slightly so she could watch him more easily. His face was faintly illuminated by the dashboard lights, throwing his strong features into relief. If anything, he looked even more handsome than he had the first time she'd seen him. Hard to believe it was only a little over five weeks ago. And look where they were now. His brows drew together slightly as he concentrated on his driving, his eyes flicking from the road to his rearview mirror and back again at regular intervals.

"Can't say anyone's ever accused me of that," he acknowledged. "Especially my father."

"Your dad's alive?" she asked, surprised. "When you didn't mention him being on the guest list today, I thought that maybe he had passed on."

"He's very much alive. Likes to think he still has a say in my life. I was relieved he couldn't make it to be honest. Dad and I rub each other the wrong way. Too much water under the bridge between us now for things to be any different."

"You don't think he'll want to be a hands-on grandfather?"

"I'm not sure I want his influence on our child. He wasn't exactly the best example of parenting back when I was a kid. How about your parents? I'm sorry they couldn't come today. Do you think they'll visit often?"

"They probably will, as much as Dad's diplomatic schedule permits. We've always been close and I'm their only child so our baby will be special to them."

She smiled softly at the memory of the joy her parents had expressed when she'd told them she was getting married. But it had been tempered with concern at her not knowing Gabe very long. But they trusted her judgment and promised to visit as soon as possible.

Gabe slowed the vehicle down and turned into his driveway before traveling up the private road that led to his house. Discreet lighting on the sides of the driveway lit the way to her future home.

The enormity of what she'd done in marrying Gabriel Carrington hit home with all the subtlety of a Texas Longhorn on a tender toe and she drew in a long breath and held it a moment before letting it go. This would all work out. It just had to. She already had the money side of their agreement and it was already in place to do good things for her business.

She was on the cusp of negotiations with a major midrange retail chain's head office with a view to introducing her leisure-wear clothing to them and branching out into her formal-wear ranges at a later stage. On the face of things, everything was working out. But tell that to the butterflies dancing in her stomach. The ones suddenly terrified by how all this would turn out.

It bothered her that Gabe had no plans to tie her to him in any way other than through their child and even then, that had been optional. It had been made patently clear that she could choose to walk away at any time. Equally clear was the directive that should she do so, Gabe would assume full custody for their child. Her lawyer had pushed back with a suggestion of shared custody but Gabe had been resolute. She knew visitation would never be enough. She already loved her baby. Because of that Ros was determined to make this marriage work, and last.

As the car approached the five-car garage, the door to one of the bays automatically opened. He drove straight in and stopped the car.

"Welcome home," he said warmly. "I hope you'll be happy here."

"Thank you," she said stiffly and undid her seat belt.

Gabe had already exited the car and was at her door before she could open it, his hand extended to help her out.

"I sent your rental back to the agency," Gabe said as she stood next to him.

"Oh, I thought I'd hold on to it a while longer."

Irritation at his high-handedness tinged her words and she was irked by the tiny smile that pulled at the corner of his mouth. The last thing she wanted was to be completely stuck here.

"Kind of unnecessary when you have a set of wheels of your own," Gabe answered her smoothly and guided her to turn around.

There in front of her was a brand-new midnight-blue Jaguar SUV with a great white satin bow tied on the hood. The inside was filled with white-and-silver balloons.

"A wedding gift," he said and reached in his pocket for a key fob, which he pressed into her hand.

Completely overwhelmed, Ros didn't know what to say or how to respond.

"You're welcome," Gabe said with an ironic twist to his mouth. "If you don't like it, I can change it for something else."

"No!" she blurted. "It's incredible. I've never owned something like this. And I feel terrible. My gift to you is tiny by comparison. I honestly don't feel I should accept this."

"You need a car and for me it's important you have something safe and reliable. We travel long distances around here and cell phone coverage can be irregular. Think of it as my peace of mind for you and the baby."

"Thank you, Gabe," she said with genuine warmth.

"We can take it out for a drive tomorrow, if you like. Get you used to the feel of it and how it handles."

"I'd like that," she said with a small smile.

Her fingers closed around the fob. Did he understand how important her independence was to her? Was that part of the reason he'd made sure she had a reliable vehicle—so she wouldn't feel trapped here by the circumstances their passion had created?

"Did you want something to eat or drink?" he asked as he started to lead her to the door to the house.

"No, I'm fine. But I wouldn't mind a shower before bed."

"Oh, I think we can do better than that. Come with me."

He led her through the house, their way lit only by subtle downlights about a foot off the floor and positioned every couple of yards along the wall. As they walked farther into the house, the lights popped on as they neared them.

"You live alone in this great big place?" she asked.

"Not anymore now you're here," he answered with a smile and a light squeeze of her hand. "My staff live in their own accommodation on the property. Cookie mostly attends to the ranch hands but makes meals for me to reheat from time to time. I don't mind cooking for myself or eating out for the balance."

He stopped outside large double wooden doors and turned to open them.

"Our suite," he said.

He drew her inside and closed the door behind them. Thick plush carpet covered the floor and the private sitting room was decorated with a large television hung on the wall over a long lightly stained wooden sideboard. Comfortable-looking dove-gray leather easy chairs bracketed a two-seater sofa, and a coffee table that matched the sideboard sat in front of them with a large bowl of fresh fruit on top. Doors led off on either side of the sitting room.

"It looks nice," she said carefully.

"It's a good place to unwind. I haven't used it much, but you're free to use it as your own retreat if you need it." He gestured to the antique desk-and-chair set over by the window. "You can use that area as your home office if you want to—we have ultra-fast internet to every room in the house. If this area isn't suitable for you, we can dedicate another room for that if you prefer more privacy. The light is very good in here during the day, so that might be helpful for your drawings."

She was surprised and warmed by his insightfulness. They hadn't even begun to discuss her workspace but it seemed he'd already thought of it.

"Thank you, I think that will do just fine for what I need." She remembered she hadn't yet given him his gift. “Do you know where I can find my things? I have something for you.”

“Of course, your room is through here.”

He led the way to one of the doors off the sitting room and opened it wide before gesturing for her to precede him. She stepped into the room and eyed the furnishings with approval. Similar to the sitting room, the predominant tones were in soft dove-gray with lightly stained washed-ash furniture. The bed was immense, and looking at it reminded her anew of the night they’d shared at her hotel, making her insides tighten on a surge of desire, her fingertips tingling with the need to touch him.

Gabe opened another set of doors that led into a massive wardrobe. Ros shifted the direction of her thoughts and looked inside. Someone, his housekeeper, she supposed, had unpacked her clothes and hung them on the rails while the drawers held her tops and undergarments and her shoes were stacked neatly on purpose-built shelves.

“Looks like you’ll need to do a bit of shopping. It’s kinda empty in here,” he teased.

“I don’t see your clothing anywhere,” she said, looking around.

“It’s in my wardrobe.”

“We’re not sharing a room?”

“I thought you might like to have your own space, while we figure this marriage thing out.”

“Oh-kay,” she said on a drawn-out breath.

This wasn’t quite the start to married life she’d

been anticipating but she was prepared to work at it. Just then she spied the wrapped gift she'd had Piers buy for Gabriel and urgent courier to her. It had arrived only this morning and she'd shoved it in her case ready to be sent to the house. Whoever had unpacked for her had left it in easy view on a small shelf in the wardrobe. She reached for it and suddenly felt horribly nervous. He'd bought her a car for goodness sake and all she had for him was this?

"I…ahh. I bought this for you, as your wedding gift. From me."

Gabe took it from her and turned it in his hand, an odd expression on his face. She began to wonder if she ought to have bothered at all, but then he looked up at her and she saw genuine gratitude on his features.

"Thank you," he said warmly.

"You don't know what it is, yet. You might not like it."

"I'm sure I'll love it. Thank you for going to the trouble of getting me something. I know these past few days have been incredibly busy for you."

His long fingers made quick work of unwrapping the box and he opened it carefully, his eyes widening as its contents were revealed. He lifted one platinum cuff link from the box and held it to the light.

"These are beautiful. I've never seen anything with such fire in it. Opals, right?"

"Yes, black opals. Symbolically they're supposed to bring good fortune and the color inside, harmony."

"A prophetic start to our marriage, then."

She hadn't meant to tell him about the symbolism behind the opals. She didn't usually believe in that stuff but it felt right and, let's face it, they needed all the help they could get.

"They're quite stunning. Thank you so much," Gabriel said and carefully put the cuff link back in its case, closed it and slipped it in his pocket. "Now, let me show you your bathroom." He led her into another room off the bedroom.

Ros was wide-eyed as she observed the massive bathroom. A three-yard-long glass-screened shower hugged one wall, adorned with multiple showerheads and a tiled seat for good measure. Certainly big enough for two, she thought, eyeing her husband. A large well-lit vanity unit with twin basins ran along the wall opposite the shower and, at the end of the room in front of floor-length glass, stood a large freestanding tub—again big enough to comfortably accommodate two.

"The glass is privacy tinted and the window looks out onto a walled courtyard so no one can see in. I could draw you a bath if you like?"

"Will you join me?"

She saw his pupils widen and his nostrils flare slightly on a sharply indrawn breath and felt a flicker of hope.

"If you want me to."

She stepped closer to him. "I do."

He took a step back. "This isn't going to be a marriage in the romantic sense, Rosalind. Just so we're clear on that."

His voice was strained and his pupils had dilated, almost consuming the darkness of his eyes. His breathing had quickened. She had no doubt he wanted her right now as much as she wanted him and her body warmed in response, her nipples growing tight and aching for his touch.

"Perfectly," she answered succinctly.

But even though she'd agreed to what he'd said, she was going to do her level best to persuade him differently. And if she couldn't use words, she'd use her body to show him what they could mean to one another.

In response, he shrugged off his jacket and his hands went to the tie at his neck, unknotting it and then swiftly yanking it from under his collar. Next, he undid the buttons of his shirt, which he discarded also before turning on the faucet over the tub. Water rippled from a waterfall-style spout and poured into the large tub. Steam quickly began to fog the window behind. Ros found herself mesmerized by the play of muscles across his back as he bent and swirled something fragrant and foamy in the water.

When he stood and returned to her, she was still frozen in place. Caught by the beauty of this man—this stranger—that she'd married. Gabe moved behind her, removed her sheer overcoat and began to undo the pearl buttons that fastened her dress down the back. One by one, slipping each from its keeper and exposing another inch of skin along the way. As he went, he pressed warm kisses to her spine, making her heart race in anticipation.

Once her dress was undone, he gently slid it from her body, leaving her standing in her heels and her underwear, which consisted of a lacy strapless bra and matching bikini undies in the palest of grays, together with matching garter belt and sheer stockings. Her legs trembled as he ran his hand down one leg and bent to remove first one shoe, then the other. Then, he unsnapped the garter loops, one by one, his fingers strong and gentle and each brush of his fingers on her skin bringing more tingling sensation to her body. Gabe gently rolled down, then removed each stocking with painstaking care before standing again and divesting himself of the rest of his clothing.

The last time she'd seen him naked had been by the dimmed light of her bedroom at the Bellamy and, to be totally honest, she hadn't been that fixated on what he looked like. Only on what he offered at the time which had been a respite from the grueling disappointments of the day. But now, she took her time to look her fill. To admire the shape of his shoulders and the latent strength visible there. To reach out and touch the breadth of his chest and smooth her palms over the sculpted shape of his muscles then the ridges of his abdomen and lower still to the well-defined V that led from his hips and arrowed to his arousal.

Boldly, she took his length in her hands, sighing a little at the heat and smoothness of his skin. It felt like forever since they'd last made love together. Every part of her thrummed to a demanding beat, wanting to touch him all over. Wanting him to touch her.

Gabriel reached around to the back of her bra and unsnapped it, tugging it away from her full and sensitive breasts and tossing the garment to one side. She felt an ache build inside her. Deeper and more insistent than the last time because this time she knew what delights awaited them both. But Gabe seemed to be content with taking his time with her tonight, and why not. They had all night and tomorrow and whatever the future held.

He removed her panties next and held her hand as she stepped free, then he led her to the tub and helped her in. The water was perfect. Not too hot, not too cold, and the silky texture of the foaming bubbles felt divine on her skin. The water rocked a little as he joined her, sliding in behind her and pulling her back against his chest. He lifted her hair and draped it over her shoulder.

"Comfortable?" he asked.

"Very, thank you. And you?"

"I'll be fine for now."

She could still feel his arousal pressed against her lower back and wondered just how comfortable he could be with her leaning against him, but she had to learn to trust him and if he said he was okay, then he must be. It felt decadent to simply lie with him like this and be supported by the warm embrace of his body and the water that surrounded them. Gabe picked up the bottle of liquid he'd added to the bath and poured a little in his hand before massaging his hands together and stroking it over her shoulders and down her arms.

The scent was slightly sweet and slightly spicy and made her feel super sexy and pampered all at the same time. Gabe continued to stroke her, from her arms now to her breasts, then her tummy and lower. The tingling sensations she had experienced before all coalesced in that one point where he touched her now.

"Okay?" he murmured against her ear.

"Better than okay. Way better," she answered and let her legs drop open farther to give him better access.

He was barely touching her but the combination of the warm water and his touch combined to have her panting in seconds as demand grew inside her.

"More, please?" she asked.

He increased the pressure of his fingers as they swirled around her most sensitive point, his other hand cupping one breast and rolling her nipple between thumb and forefinger. She let her head drop back against the solid strength of his shoulder and gave herself over to the sensations that poured through her, rode each wave as it intensified until she suddenly crested—a gasp of sheer delight escaping her as she orgasmed.

Gabe continued to hold her to him. Never before had she felt so protected and satiated at the same time. It was a feeling she could definitely get used to. But what of their marriage? What they shared physically was without par but marriage needed more than sex to survive. Could she hope that maybe they'd become friends, and more, as time progressed? He'd said no romance and he'd been adamant about that. And she'd accepted it, but now she began to wonder if this incendiary connection they had would be enough. If *she* would be enough.

Six

It had been only two days since he and Rosalind had married. Two days where they'd barely left the master suite except to grab some food and drink from time to time. He thought he'd sated himself on her after their wedding night but it appeared he only continued to want her more. And wanted to please her more, too.

It was a worrying trend. He hadn't expected to find himself thinking about her all the time, nor wanting to be with her as much, either. Even today, a day where he was calling on one of Royal's oldest inhabitants before he was scheduled to meet his father for lunch, he'd suggested Ros drive them in her new car. He'd told himself it was because she needed the experience, but he knew it had more to do with his inability to be apart from her for too long.

Gabe directed Ros to turn into the next driveway so he could introduce her to Emmalou Hilliard. The retired cowgirl was still fierce about living independently at the ripe age of ninety-nine years old. He'd invited Emmalou to attend the wedding reception at the club, offering to arrange transport, but she'd refused citing her arthritis in the colder weather making it painful for her to do much more than be in her favorite armchair at home. But she'd insisted on meeting his new bride and invited them to call in at their earliest convenience.

"Are you sure she won't mind us dropping in like this?" Ros asked as she brought the car to a halt outside the old lady's home.

"She'll love it, especially since she gets to meet you before a lot of the other residents around Royal."

He linked his hand with Ros's as they alighted from the car and they approached the front door of the tiny four-room cottage where Emmalou lived alone. Others had suggested she'd be better off at an elder care facility but she stubbornly refused to move. That said, she had accepted help in the form of a cleaner who visited once a week and a team who brought nutritious meals to ensure she kept up her strength.

"Tell me again how you know her?" Ros asked as they approached the front steps.

"Emmalou was one of the early cowgirls in the

area. She worked for a lady rancher, Violetta Ford. They were apparently quite a formidable team."

"And this Violetta Ford, I heard someone say at the reception that she left town after some stink about not being able to join the cattleman's club and followed her family back East?"

"Yeah, the same family who'd decided she was an embarrassment to them with her demands to join the club. She ended up selling her ranch to a guy named Vincent Fenwick. By all accounts he was a good rancher. Kept Emmalou on, too, which was forward-thinking of him for the time."

"Well, if she'd already proven herself as a good hand and had a strong working knowledge of the ranch, it would have made sense to keep her, surely."

"Yeah, but times were different then. In fact, it's only in the last ten years that the club allowed women to be members. Apparently, that was something Violetta was very hot under the collar about. When she started the ranch a lot of people laughed at her for being so bold as to step into what was considered very much a man's world, despite the fact ranchers' wives were always busy on the land, too. Despite the lack of support, she made it a success and felt she deserved membership with the club as much as any other rancher did. Regrettably, the old-school good old boys did not." He looked up at the house and smiled. "There's Emmalou now."

The old lady stood on her front porch and bellowed at them. "Are you two gonna stand about all day out there? Come in. You're makin' me let all the heat out!"

"Be right there, Miss Emmalou," Gabe said.

They ascended the stairs and he paused to introduce Rosalind.

"Miss Emmalou, this is my wife, Rosalind Banks."

"Banks, huh? Not taking your name, then? Given your family, I can understand that," she said bluntly with a finger poke at his chest. Emmalou turned and faced Rosalind and looked her up and down. "Yep, you look like you've got staying power. You're gonna need it with this one. I've known him since he was little more than a twinkle in his daddy's eye. He's always been a handful. You'll need to keep your wits about you."

"Thank you for the advice, Ms. Hilliard."

"Call me Emmalou or Miss Emmalou. None of that Ms. rubbish. I made my choice to remain a spinster and I'm proud of it. No shame in being Miss anything."

Gabe fought a smile as he watched the look of bewilderment take over Ros's features. Emmalou turned around and stomped back into the house.

"Well, come on! You don't wanna keep an old lady on the porch in this cold, do ya?"

Ros bent her head in Gabe's direction. "Is she always like this?"

He grinned back. "Yeah, priceless, huh?"

They followed Emmalou inside and sat exactly where she told them.

"That's it," she said as Ros settled in a chair bathed in the morning light. "Can I get you two any coffee?"

"Not for me, thank you," Ros replied.

"Ros would prefer an herbal tea if you have one. I would love a black coffee."

"I'll see what I can find. People are always bringing round baskets of all manner of things for me. Can't stand most of it but it keeps the cupboards full."

She stomped toward the back of the tiny house and they could hear her muttering as cupboard doors were opened and banged closed again.

Gabe laughed. "I forgot how she can be so blunt. I should have known better. She's always been a pistol."

"Is that what you call it?" Ros said, raising one brow. "She's an original—that's for sure."

After a few moments, Emmalou came back into the sitting room, pushing a small tea trolley set with a lace doily, cups and saucers and a plate of cookies arranged on top. Gabe shot to his feet to aid her.

"No, no, young Gabriel. I can manage just fine, thank you. Used to be I could carry all this on a tray but my balance ain't so grand these days. Getting old is a bitch but it sure beats the alternative!" She cackled a laugh again. "Now, Rosalind, I found some red bush tea in the back of the cupboard. Smells good so I hope it's good for you. Gabriel, here's your coffee."

She handed the hot drinks and then the plate around before settling into her chair. Gabe could almost swear he heard her bones creak.

"Tell me about yourself, Rosalind. Gabriel, here, tells me you're a dressmaker?"

Ros smiled. "Kind of like that. I head up my own fashion brand in Australia and we distribute worldwide. Currently I'm aiming to branch into the market here in America."

"Australia, you say. You got cowgirls there, too, right?"

"Yes, we call them jillaroos."

"Jillaroos, I like that." Emmalou nodded. She turned her attention to Gabe. "Have you met that pesky reporter? What's her name…sounds like a mountain range. Yeah, that's right. Sierra something or other."

"Has she been bothering you?" Gabe asked, ready to do battle if necessary.

"Nothing I can't handle. She was asking about Violetta. I told her she was a good boss until she left and then I just kept on working for the guy who took over the ranch. She kept pestering me about whether or not I knew anything about some danged secret baby Violetta was supposed to have had. Frankly, I told her to mind her own business and leave the past where it lay. She didn't much like that."

"She wouldn't," Gabe said darkly. "About a month ago she asked me if I thought a Carrington could have been Harmon Wentworth's daddy. Ms. Morgan's mind sure goes on tangents."

"I promised Violetta I'd never tell a soul her secrets and she always told me everything. Said it was better than confession, ha! She had one helluva secret, excuse my language."

"And did she tell you that secret?" Ros asked, suddenly fiercely curious.

Emmalou nodded slowly. "She did, but that's in the vault. I ain't telling nobody what she entrusted me with, and that's that. And I know for darn sure she never slept with no Carrington," Emmalou said adamantly.

Which begged the question, did she know if Violetta had slept with someone else? Maybe Emmalou knew a great deal more than she was letting on. One thing was for sure, though. If Sierra Morgan's theories had any basis in fact, she wouldn't be finding that out from Emmalou. The old woman had held her secrets this long; she wasn't about to change now.

They visited a while longer before Emmalou appeared to tire. Gabe stood and reloaded the tea trolley with their cups and the cookie plate and took them through to the kitchen.

"Just leave 'em be," Emmalou called to him from the sitting room. "I'll get to 'em later. Give me something to look forward to."

"If you say so," Gabe said, returning to the sitting room. "Thank you for having us to visit."

"You know you don't need to stand on ceremony

with me, boy. Call in any time. You, too," she said, directing her attention to Rosalind. "And take care of each other, y'hear."

"We will," Gabe assured her. "Don't get up. We'll see ourselves out."

"Thank you for the tea, Miss Emmalou," Ros added. "It's been lovely meeting you."

"Nice manners, that one," Emmalou said to Gabe. "You'd better keep your nose clean and hold on to her."

"Yes, ma'am."

They left the old lady sitting in her chair and once they were in the car, Ros turned to Gabe.

"What is that business you two were talking about with her old boss?"

"Just some rumor that's started up. Carson Wentworth's great-grandfather, Harmon, believes he was adopted as a baby, although there are no records to support his claim. A female photojournalist named Arielle Martin who visited Royal last year did some investigating and seemed to think that Violetta was likely his birth mom. It's all conjecture."

"What does that have to do with the reporter?"

"Ms. Morgan is like a dog with a bone on the subject. Thinks she can scent a news story there. It's upset a lot of people and threatens what we've all accepted and believed to be the truth for four generations, not to mention tears the very fabric of the founders of the Texas Cattleman's Club to shreds. She's gotten a hold of Arielle's diary and is following up on what she discovered and is trying to find out who Violetta may have had an affair with. Hell, it all happened a hundred years ago." He shook his head. "The past is best left there."

"Well, at least you know that your family isn't part of it," Ros commented.

"Yeah, there is that."

Ros dropped Gabe off at the RCW Steakhouse where he was supposed to meet his dad. Denver Carrington had been quite specific that he only wished to see Gabe. Gabe had been tempted to tell him to go to hell but Ros had encouraged him to talk to his father and said it would be a good time for her to look around the town while they had lunch. She planned to drive out to the Courtyard shops to browse the antiques shop and crafts studio there. On her return to town she had arranged a meeting with the proprietor of Natalie Valentine's Bridal Shop, with a view to providing some of her evening wear that would work as mother-of-the-bride-or-groom garments, to supplement the range already stocked there.

He admired Ros's drive to look for new opportunities and outlets for her designs. Her mind was constantly working. What he didn't admire, however, was his new and constant need to touch her, or be in the same space as her. Or be thinking about her when he should be doing something else. Like how he was going to get through this lunch with his father without losing his temper as he usually did.

Gabe walked into the RCW Steakhouse and spied his father at his usual table near the back of the restaurant. His father sat there, reading something on his phone, as if he had not a care in the world. Gabe wished he could say the same.

"Dad," he acknowledged as he approached the table.

His father stood and shook his hand. "Congratulations on your marriage, son."

"I thought you'd have wanted to meet my wife. Why didn't you include Ros in your invitation?"

"Can you blame a father for wanting a little one-on-one time with his son?" Denver said with a feeble attempt to look affronted.

"You've never been keen on spending time with me before, why start now?"

"Son, can we put your bitterness toward me aside for an hour or two? If you keep this up, we'll both end up with indigestion. Anyway, I want to say I'm sorry I couldn't make it to your reception."

Gabe had learned many years ago not to expect his father to make it to anything that was important to him. Not high school prize giving, not college graduation. Nothing.

"I saw a picture of your wife in the local paper. Pretty girl."

Even when paying a compliment his dad still managed to be condescending. Gabe counted to three before responding.

"Rosalind is a successful businesswoman. Not

only is she incredibly talented in her field, but she's also extremely beautiful. I'm quite sure that *pretty* doesn't exactly cover it."

"Noted," his dad said with a smirk.

Gabe knew he shouldn't have risen to his father's bait, especially not with the number of restaurant patrons with their heads now turned their way.

"It helps if they're pretty, though," his father continued. "Especially if they're good in the sack. Makes a marriage last longer. I hope you have a watertight prenup set up. Wouldn't do to let a stranger get her hands on what's yours."

Gabe didn't respond to his father's crude comments. When Denver had finally left Gabe's mom, after years of cheating on her, he'd married again, only to cheat on that wife with the third Mrs. Carrington. His father was hardly an authority on the subject of a lasting marriage. He'd left each successive wife with little more than enough money to survive on, something that had driven Gabe to ensure he never relied on his father for anything.

He busied himself with studying the menu when he became aware of someone approaching their table. Sienna Morgan. Again. The woman was as dogged as they came.

"Gentlemen," she said in acknowledgement as they both rose to greet her. "Please, sit down. I won't take much of your time."

"Ms. Morgan," Gabe's dad said with barely concealed dislike. "As you can see, my son and I are enjoying a private lunch together and would prefer to keep it that way. Private. I would also like to state for the record that you have been categorically told by myself and my father that my grandfather did not have an affair with Violetta Ford. If you continue to pursue that line of questioning with us, you will find a lawsuit on your hands."

"Oh, I'm not here to question you," the reporter said staunchly. "In fact, I just wanted to let you know that I've had confirmation that it wasn't a Carrington who had the affair with Violetta."

Gabe spoke up, deciding to take a different tack to his father's threats. "Ms. Morgan, I know you've been to see Emmalou Hilliard. I'd be grateful if you wouldn't bother her again."

"Bother her? I was only asking her to tell me about the good old days. She's bound to have some great stories about when she and Violetta Ford ran the Ford ranch. And Miss Hilliard is likely the only person left alive who can maybe put Harmon Wentworth's mind at rest about his true parentage. Don't you think Harmon has a right to that?"

There was an edge to Sierra Morgan's voice that told Gabe she was none too happy to be told to stay away from one of the only people still alive who'd known Violetta Ford.

"You might never uncover the truth behind Harmon's parentage and all this poking around other people's lives is causing tension. Is that your goal?" Denver Carrington snapped at Sienna Morgan.

"There's a story here—I know it. And if revealing the dirty secrets of Royal's elite is what it takes, then that's what I'll do."

Denver scoffed. "Sensationalism to sell more papers, more like. Now, is there anything else?"

"No, not at the moment," she said with a forced smile.

"Good, then perhaps you'll leave us to our lunch," he said dismissing her.

She nodded before pivoting on her heels and walking away from them.

"Not a fan of Ms. Morgan, then?" Gabe remarked.

"She's a reporter. I don't trust 'em and see no reason to encourage 'em. She's pretty enough, sure, but she certainly doesn't know her place. Now, what are you choosing today? It's my treat."

"Thank you, I'll go with the house special."

Denver looked up at the waiter who'd approached their table the moment the reporter had left. "Make that two house specials, and a bottle of your finest merlot to go along with it."

"Just mineral water for me," Gabe said firmly.

"Oh yeah, I forgot. You're on honeymoon. Need to keep your wits about you, eh? A half bottle then," Denver amended. "So, have you heard any other news lately?"

"Carson told me Harmon announced that unless someone solves the mystery of who his parents truly were and the feuding between the Wentworths and the Langleys stops, he won't leave a red cent to the Texas Cattleman's Club."

"What? That's just wrong! Nothing matters more than that money in the club's coffers. Maybe that reporter-gal needs to get busy after all."

Not for the first time Gabe realized that his father's concern, first and foremost, was always money. And he might have agreed with him up to a point, except these past days with Rosalind had taught him something else—that other things mattered too, like people and relationships. Gabe felt a shock wave plummet through him at the thought. He'd believed he'd inured himself to the concept of love and happy-ever-after but here he was, wanting to tell his father that money wasn't the be-all and end-all of everything.

"What's the matter, son? You look like you swallowed a fly," Denver said with a bark of laughter.

"Nothing," Gabe said.

But it wasn't nothing. It was anything but. He was developing feelings for his wife. Feelings he hadn't counted on. Feelings he hadn't wanted, period. What the hell was he going to do about that? A spark of interest in the back of his mind told him he ought to simply relax and go with the flow, but then his more pragmatic side kicked in. He was the one who'd set the boundaries of his marriage to Rosalind. She'd agreed to them. Sex, well, that was an unexpected bonus but now that she was pregnant with his baby it wasn't absolutely necessary and, frankly, it was clouding the issue of the parameters of their arrangement. If they continued to sleep together, Gabe would continue to confuse sex with the messy feelings that were already intruding on him. Which was exactly what he'd expected to happen, but with Rosalind, not with him.

The sex had to stop.

Every cell in his body reeled in protest but the more he thought about it, the more he knew that was the road he needed to take. He needed to ensure that he held strong to his reasons for keeping his heart out of this. Looking at his father was a good incentive. He had no wish to become like him—to be responsible for the unnecessary hurt and pain caused to others with his selfish actions. The best way to do that was not to fall in love, nor to allow anyone else to fall in love with him. With the exception of his child, of course. For his son or daughter he would be the perfect loving father, completely the opposite of the example that had been given to him.

Their lunches arrived and Gabe applied himself to the meal with the concentration of an accountant with a spreadsheet. Anything to keep his mind on track and off Rosalind.

Seven

Ros left the bridal boutique with a new spring in her step. She'd had a lovely morning out at the Courtyard shops and a very promising meeting with Natalie Valentine who owned the bridal shop. Natalie had been enthusiastic about Ros's designs for special-occasion wear and had asked to see samples. Natalie had said that she lost a lot of formal-wear business to the major city boutiques because she simply didn't have the range here in her own store. With the Texas Cattleman's Club featuring so hugely in town and with the many formal and informal occasions it hosted, the demand for quality formal wear was a constant among the women in the area. It would be a win-win for both Ros and Natalie if they could work together on a suitable line to offer to the women of Royal.

Now all Ros had to do was get said samples promptly sent over here. She made a note in her phone to follow up with Piers.

Her tummy growled, reminding her she hadn't had lunch yet. There were several places she could buy something to eat in Royal but Natalie had spoken highly of the Royal Diner. It wasn't too far from here but the wind outside was freezing so, remembering the instructions Natalie had given her, Ros drove there. Luckily there was a parking spot right outside. She went in and was delighted to discover the interior had a very retro 1950s feel about it with red faux-leather booths and a black-and-white linoleum floor.

"Where's Fonzie?" she muttered aloud as she made her way to an empty booth and settled there. She hadn't been seated long when a server came over.

"Hi, I'm Amanda Battle, the proprietor here. You're new in town, right?"

"Yes, Rosalind Banks."

"Say, aren't you the girl who married Gabriel Carrington a few days ago?"

"The one and the same," Ros said with a smile.

Seemed news traveled fast around here. She'd had a similar response from just about everyone she'd met in and around town today.

"Welcome and congratulations! But where's your

new husband? Don't tell me he's left you to your own devices already!" Amanda Battle looked shocked.

"He had a meeting with his father so I'm flying solo today."

"Well, that explains it, then." Amanda smiled and passed Ros a menu. "Everything's good today but I have to say the chef's special, mac 'n' cheese, is sublime."

"I'll have that then," Ros said with a smile. "With a small green salad on the side, please."

"Coffee?"

Ros felt her stomach lurch at the thought. "No thank you. Mineral water, please."

"I'll send one of the girls over with your water in a moment. And, if you need a friend or just someone to talk to, you pop on by, y'hear? I imagine you don't know that many people here yet."

"Thank you, that's lovely of you."

Ros felt the sting of tears at the woman's kindness. The sense of isolation she'd felt when she'd left Gabe to meet his father had surprised her. She hadn't felt that way in New York, maybe because she remembered it from when she lived there with her parents, but in this town where everyone seemed to know everyone else, she felt like a rank outsider.

The food, when it came, was filling and wholesome and Ros left a generous tip with her payment as she exited her booth. She'd seen a few people she recognized from the wedding reception come and go while she was there and they'd acknowledged her with a nod, but for the most part she'd been left alone. As she got back in her car her phone rang. She used the hands-free option on the vehicle to answer and felt an unaccustomed surge of relief when she heard Gabe's voice.

"How're you doing?" he asked.

"I've had a good time—how about you?"

"I had lunch with my father."

"So not a great time then?"

"You could say that. He's not the easiest man to get along with."

"Would you like me to pick you up now?"

"Actually, I have a little business here in town. Do you think you can find your own way back to the ranch?"

She felt a surprising pang of disappointment, but then rallied her senses. It was a reasonable request, after all.

"I'm sure I'll be fine," she said firmly. "How will you get back?"

"I'll figure something out," he said vaguely.

"I can wait around town, find something else to do until you're finished," she said helpfully.

"No. I have no idea how long I'll be. Best you head back to the ranch. I'll see you there around dinnertime."

And with that, he severed the call. No goodbye. No indication of what time dinner actually was. If the past few nights had been anything to go by, it could be anywhere between six and ten o'clock.

Ros stared blindly out the windshield of her car. There'd been a different tone in his voice than when they parted. As if being apart had created a distance between them. The warmth that she'd grown accustomed to hearing when he spoke to her was gone. Not that he was rude, just detached. If that was what having lunch with his father did for him, she'd have to encourage him not to see his dad often, at all.

She started up her car and slipped it into gear and pulled out into the street.

"Who needs GPS?" she said to herself. "It'll be an adventure to find my own way back. How hard could it be in a place like this?"

Harder than she imagined, she discovered. She was glad for the full tank of gas in the car because she had to backtrack several times during her journey back to the ranch. But she knew she was on the right track when she drove past Emmalou's place. A curl of smoke drifted from the brick chimney and lights glowed from inside the tiny home. Seeing the lights in the windows made Ros realize just how long she'd been driving around. It had been several hours since she'd had lunch and she was beginning to feel ravenously hungry again. Still, she consoled herself, not far to go now.

By the time she pulled up in her bay in the garage, she was feeling the effects of that hunger combined with the hours of concentration and driving. Weariness pulled at every muscle in her body as she alighted from the car and her bladder was none too happy about the length of time it had been since her last toilet stop back at the diner.

"Where the hell have you been? You should have been back hours ago," Gabe demanded, looming from what felt like out of nowhere.

"I beg your pardon?"

This was a side of him she hadn't seen before and it was a stark reminder of how little she actually knew him. Oh sure, she knew how to make his entire body tense with anticipation and she knew how to make him growl with impatience as she took her time exploring that same body. But as to what made him tick, she knew very little.

"I got sidetracked when I took a wrong turn."

"You didn't use the GPS?" he demanded.

"I didn't think it would be that hard to find my way back, but turned out my sense of direction isn't that great when it comes to the back end of nowhere."

She couldn't help that last statement. She had been nervous when she'd lost her way more than once and hadn't been able to figure out using the GPS.

"Rosalind, this isn't the city where everything is laid out in blocks and there's someone to give you directions on virtually every corner. We're out on the range, here. A long way from town or help. Plus, there are areas where there is no phone coverage. You took a serious risk doing what you did, especially at this time of year. You could have put both yourself and the baby in danger. Don't be so reckless next time. The car is fitted with an excellent GPS—use it."

With that he turned sharply and stalked away, leaving Ros to stare at his retreating back feeling a mixture of shock and irritation. How dare he speak to her like that? Her hands curled into tight fists of frustration, at him and at herself for not standing up and telling him she'd do what she damn well pleased when it came to driving around. She started after him but changed her mind partway, deciding that giving him a piece of her mind while she was angry was probably not the best course of action.

This whole marriage thing was painfully new to them both and they needed to work at it much harder than she'd realized. It was all very well to spend their nights together, exploring all the things that made their bodies sing in perfect harmony, but they needed to find a middle ground where they could be friends during the day, as well.

After going to the bathroom, Ros detoured to the kitchen, where she discovered a covered plate in the oven. Just the one serving, which told her he'd obviously eaten alone while waiting for her return. She shrugged out of her coat and set it and her bag on a chair at the breakfast bar before getting herself some cutlery and bringing her plate from the oven to sit in splendid isolation at the granite counter and eat her meal. She was partway through when she heard a sound in the doorway. She looked up to see Gabe standing there, watching her.

"I was worried about you," he said bluntly.

"As you can see, I'm just fine, but thank you for caring."

His face tightened and he took a step forward. "I meant it when I said it—you took a serious risk. Anything could have happened to you."

"Like what, being mooed to death by a cow?"

"Like getting stuck on the side of the road with no phone reception and the temperatures dropping. Like running out of gas and not being able to keep the heater in your car running. Like an unexpected snowfall burying you in a drift before anyone could come along and find you."

She put up a hand. "Okay, okay. I get it. I'll use the GPS in future. I promise. I honestly didn't think it'd be that hard to find my way back. Usually, my sense of direction is excellent."

"But it wasn't today."

"No," she conceded. "It wasn't. I'm sorry I worried you."

"I'm sorry I raised my voice."

Silence fell between them for a full minute before Gabe spoke again.

"Rosalind, it's imperative you do everything you can to keep our baby safe—you know that, don't you?"

She flinched as though he'd slapped her. Really? Was that what all this was about? It really had nothing to do with him caring whether she froze on the side of the road or not. It was all about his darned heir. She'd thought they were making some progress in this crazy mixed-up relationship of theirs. They'd managed to be in agreement on every carefully constructed point in the contract they'd both signed prior to their wedding. They'd had the kind of wedding night that she'd always dreamed of even if their reasons for marriage hadn't involved love.

She knew they could make this work. But that would only happen if they were both equally invested in doing so. It seemed he hadn't been kidding when he said he only wanted a wife so he could have an heir. She just hadn't realized what that entailed.

"I knew I had plenty of gas. I wasn't in danger. And I object to you treating me like a child. You forget, while I was born here in America, I've spent many, many years in Australia, too. The Australian Outback is equally as challenging as your Texas ranges. Possibly even more so."

"But you weren't pregnant with my baby when you were in Australia, were you?"

His words took the wind right out of her. Why, why, why had she become pregnant? Her low-dose pill had never let her down before and she was accustomed to travel. So why this, why now, why *him*?

She looked down at the plate of food she'd been eating, suddenly losing all appetite. She got up and took her plate to the trash bin and scraped the contents into it before rinsing and stacking her plate and implements in the dishwasher.

"Did you have enough to eat?"

"I'm not hungry anymore. In fact, I think I'll head off to bed. Good night."

Gabe watched as she grabbed her coat and bag and headed toward the hall that led to the bedroom. Instinct urged him to go after her. To soothe the anger that he'd seen flash in her blue eyes. He'd knew he'd been over-the-top with his response, and while he'd told her it was because he'd been worried for the baby he knew it was far more.

He hadn't been able to get her out of his mind but he couldn't tell her that. It was contrary to everything he'd stipulated about their marriage. It had been easier to focus on the baby's safety than admit that his feelings for her were changing and growing, as hard as he fought against them, and he'd been terrified something had happened to her.

He took a step to follow her then drew himself up again.

Lunch with his father had reminded him of all the reasons why he hadn't pursued a normal marriage. He didn't want the complications that came with it or the hurt that came when it became clear the other person did not love as much as you did. Seeing his mother crushed by his father's cheating had left deep scars on his heart and her death in a car wreck not too long after he'd left them had added to them.

While the head-on collision with a drug-affected driver had clearly been out of his mother's control, he couldn't help but wonder in the years since that if she'd been in a better frame of mind would she have noticed the car barreling toward her earlier and been able to take evasive action? His gut clenched at the thought of something like that having happened to Ros today. A pain not unlike that he'd experienced after his mom's death shafted through him, robbing him of breath.

He reached a hand to the countertop, steadying himself. And reminded himself Ros had been fine. Lost, but fine. And she'd found her way home eventually. His night would not end the same way that it had so many years ago.

Gabe and his mom had lived alone after his father had walked out to set up house with his latest love interest. Waiting for her to come home that night was still vivid in his mind. She'd been assisting with putting up decorations for a fundraiser at the Texas Cattleman's Club the next day. Even though the cops had told him she hadn't stood a chance when the other vehicle had crossed in her path, he still wondered. Gabe clenched his hands into fists. He would not let the fear and grief of that night be repeated.

Later, he entered their bedroom suite to find the sitting room in complete darkness. The last few nights they'd gone to bed together and it already felt foreign to him to come into the suite alone. He found himself standing in front of her bedroom door without even realizing he'd walked there. No light shone around the edges. She was very obviously in bed already. Asleep? He wondered.

He pressed his hand against the door as if he could feel her consciousness then uttered a small sound of disgust at himself. He was behaving like some lovelorn fool when love didn't even enter into the equation with the kind of marriage they had. Nor would it.

Gabe turned sharply and headed to his bedroom on the other side of the sitting room and got ready for bed. But hours later he found himself still staring at the ceiling, his arms empty and with an indefinable ache at the center of his chest. He rolled onto his side and punched his pillow into shape. He couldn't miss something he'd never had and never wanted, he reminded himself.

But even though he told himself this, it was almost dawn before he drifted off to sleep.

The next morning, he rose later than usual, feeling groggy from the combination of lack of sleep and the too deep sleep he'd finally succumbed to. He showered quickly and dressed in jeans and a flannel shirt. It was time to show Ros around the ranch. Not on horseback, which was his preferred method of transport around the ranch, but on one of the four-by-fours he kept in the shed for the ranch hands to use while rounding up.

It was quiet on the ranch this time of year, with stock moved in closer to the buildings. They'd experimented with calving a number of their cows in the fall and he wanted to ensure the supplemental feeding regime to keep the herd healthy and ensure the best prices for the calves come spring was doing everything they'd hoped for. He also hoped that Ros would enjoy the trip out to see the cows and their calves, but realized he knew so little about her that he had no idea if she even had a pair of boots suitable for walking out on the pasture.

She wasn't in the kitchen when he got there, but a few crumbs on the countertop gave evidence that she'd had something to eat already. Probably not enough to eat, if her lack of appetite lately was anything to go by. He knew she suffered from nausea from time to time and it worried him that pregnancy was making her uncomfortable. She had enough to get used to right now without adding feeling sick into the bargain.

Gabe checked the other rooms of the house but couldn't find any trace of her until he caught a glimpse of light at the end of the hall that led to the garage. He followed the light and was surprised to find her in her car staring intently at the dash and tapping on the screen with an increasing look of irritation on her face.

"Problem?" he asked, standing by the open car door.

She jumped visibly. "Jeez, Gabe. Talk about scare a girl to death."

"Sorry, you looked like you were having trouble."

"I'm trying to figure out the GPS. If I save this point, I should be able to navigate back here from wherever I end up at any stage, right?"

"That's the theory. You want me to give it a try?"

"I wanted to work this out for myself, but whatever."

She sounded utterly defeated. Gabe walked around to the passenger side of the car, settled in the seat and looked at the screen. An error message flashed determinedly, preventing the input of any new data.

"First, we need to clear the message."

"Really? You think I don't know that? You must think I'm an absolute fool," she said in a withering tone.

"I don't think you're a fool and I'm sorry if I made you feel that way last night. I was worried about you."

"You didn't have to worry."

He knew that unless he opened up a bit, she'd never understand why he'd been so anxious.

"Look, I respect that you feel that way, but I lost my mom when she was involved in a crash on the road home one night. I waited and waited but she never arrived."

He heard Ros's sharply indrawn breath. "Oh, Gabe. I'm so sorry. I had no idea."

He shrugged. "It was a long time ago but when I'm expecting someone, I tend to be a clock watcher. Add to the equation that you're unfamiliar with the roads around here and that you're probably used to driving on the other side of the road—"

"You don't have to say any more. Honestly, it's

why I'm here trying to set this darn thing up correctly in the first place. Except all I seem to be able to get is that."

She gestured to the error message on the screen.

"Let's see if we can fix this together. Have you checked the owner's manual?"

She rolled her eyes. "No, I haven't. Shouldn't this kind of thing be simple and intuitive?"

He grinned back at her. "Well, I've always found that when simple and intuitive fails, it pays to check the manual."

"Seriously? A man who uses a manual?" she asked incredulously.

"Well don't tell everybody or I'll lose my man-card," he said with a quick grin.

She smiled back at him and he felt as if he'd been rewarded with a gold star. The tension inside him begin to ease. He popped the glove compartment open and extracted the manual.

"How about I read the instructions out loud and you do the programming, that way you'll get more familiar with what menu selections to choose?"

After a few minutes they had several destinations programmed into the GPS and Ros was satisfied that she could operate the functions without any problems.

"Okay, it looks like you're all set up."

"Thank you, it was driving me crazy."

"You'd have figured it out eventually. Do you have

plans for today?" he asked. "I was hoping to show you around the ranch, if you're okay with that."

"What do I need to wear?" she asked.

"You'll need a thick, warm coat and boots and a few layers of warm clothing. Oh, and a hat if you have one. Wool would be best, but any kind of beanie will do."

She pulled a face. "I don't think I packed anything like that. I was planning to be in New York, not the back end of civilization."

While she laughed as she said it, he couldn't help but be offended. They might be remote here on the ranch but it was hardly the back end of civilization. But then she was unashamedly a city girl. Maybe when she understood more about the ranch, and the running of it, she'd have more appreciation for things out here.

"No problem, you can wear one of my beanies and I know I have a spare jacket you can borrow. It'll swim on you but you'll be warm."

"Okay, warm is good. Come on then, let's go gear up and you can show me your ranch."

She looked eager to see what his world entailed and that ignited an unexpected spark of hope within him. One he rapidly dashed. He didn't want hope when it came to Rosalind. He just wanted an amicable relationship where they raised a child together. Was that too much to ask?

Eight

Ros felt grossly cumbersome dressed in Gabe's sheepskin-lined coat as they walked out the back of the ranch house and toward the stables and outbuildings. A light sprinkling of snow was already melting on the ground and her boots were more suitable for hard pavements than the rapidly forming mud that was beneath her feet right now. She felt herself start to slip but Gabe was quick to catch her with one arm around her waist.

"Thanks," she said, gratefully. "If we're going to do this kind of thing more often, I'm going to need to invest in a better pair of boots. Does it snow here a lot?"

"This is about as much snow as we're going to get

this winter. Are you warm enough? We can go back inside if you think you'll be too cold."

He sounded disappointed and she wanted to make it up to him for the misunderstanding over her being so late last night. If she'd have known about the situation with his mom, she would have called him. There was no way—even if her toes were already likely turning blue in her fashionable but synthetic socks—that she was going to turn him down now.

"I'm fine. Really," she said, attempting to inject as much enthusiasm as she could into her voice. She looked at the stables they were walking toward. "We're not going on horseback, are we? I might have neglected to tell you, I can't ride."

"After the baby is born we can remedy that. I have plenty of gentle-natured horses you can choose from."

"I also neglected to tell you that I'm terrified of the beasts. One end for biting, the other for kicking, right?"

He laughed and she felt herself light up inside at the sound.

"Yeah, something like that, with the ornery ones anyway. But my horses are gently bred and kindly raised and trained. You generally won't see a nip or a kick out of them. Come on in and meet them."

He guided her to the main entrance of the stables and swung the massive wooden door open. She was assailed with warmth the moment she stepped in, along with an array of scents of sweet hay, oats, wood, leather and horses. Gabe closed the door behind them. The scents grew stronger.

"Is it temperature controlled in here?" she asked, beginning to feel warmer straightaway.

But with feeling warmer, also came a sense of being overwhelmed by the smells and the heat, all combining to make a swell of nausea rise within her. She determinedly swallowed against it.

"Yes, these are working animals and we need to keep them at their peak at all times."

One horse, with its head hanging out of a nearby stall, whickered softly as Gabe came closer. She watched carefully as he stepped toward the animal and put a hand to its head, then his forehead to the horse's, as well. She heard him murmur something softly, the sound little more than a deep rumble and, as if the horse agreed with him, it nodded gently.

"Communing with nature?" she asked, staying well and truly back.

"Sure, come on over. You can give Ulysses a treat."

"Do I have to?" she said with a small laugh to conceal her nerves.

"He won't hurt you I promise."

She forced herself to put one foot in front of the other until she was level with Gabe. The horse lifted his head and looked at her as if he were sizing her up for his next meal. The nauseous sensation grew stronger.

"Gabe, I—"

"Here." He took a small carrot from his pocket and pressed it in her hand. "Hold it out like this."

He demonstrated with his own empty hand held out flat, palm up. Ulysses nuzzled Gabe's empty palm and tossed his head in disappointment.

"Your turn," he encouraged.

Ros forced herself to uncurl her fingers and held out the carrot on her palm, as Gabe had shown her. Ulysses wasted no time checking it out. She flinched as his mouth nuzzled her hand. Soft, she realized, and incredibly gentle. Finding the carrot, Ulysses snatched it up in his teeth and chomped happily. Ros took a step back, a rush of adrenaline coursing through her. She'd done it. She'd fed a carrot to a horse. She should feel elated; instead she just wanted to be sick.

She couldn't hold the nausea at bay any longer and headed for the door.

"I'm sorry, I need some fresh air," she managed before pushing open the stable door and staggering outside where she promptly lost what was left of her breakfast.

This was worse than the other times she'd been sick. So much worse. The smell of the stable continued to wrap around her like a thick miasma until she was vaguely aware of Gabe coming through the door, closing it firmly behind him.

"Ros, are you okay?"

"No, I think I need to lie down for a bit. Can we postpone today's tour for another time?"

She turned abruptly away from him and dry retched some more.

"I'll call the doctor," he said, stepping forward and taking her by the arm.

"No need. Just morning sickness. It should pass, I hope."

"If it doesn't I'm taking you to the doctor, no arguments."

"Fine," she said, feeling too weak right now to argue.

Gabe walked her back inside the house and bent to remove her boots and helped her out of the heavy jacket before taking her to her room. He pushed back the covers of the freshly made bed while she went to the bathroom to brush her teeth again and when she returned, she gratefully lay down and put her head on her pillow. She felt utterly wretched and exhausted.

"I'll be fine in a bit. Just let me get some sleep. The sickness seems to be worse if I get overtired."

"You didn't sleep well last night?" he said, concern obvious in every line of his face.

"Not particularly."

He pulled the covers over her and hovered, obviously unsure of what to do next.

"Can I get you anything?"

"No, thank you."

He turned to go but was stopped by her calling his name.

"Gabe?"

"Do you need something?"

"Will you lie with me?"

He felt torn. Every instinct told him to climb into the bed with her but he had to draw a line somewhere and that line was drawn here and now.

"No, I need to go out on the ranch for a while but I'll stay within easy reach of the house. Phone me if you need me, all right? And I'll ask Doreen to check on you in a short while. And, Ros, I think it's best if we don't sleep together anymore. It's confusing things."

"This is just a bit of morning sickness," she argued.

"Whatever, you need your rest and we need to keep to the terms of the contract."

She closed her eyes then, her fingers clutching the sheets tight around her. "Right, the contract."

Gabe left her room and closed the door quietly behind him. She'd looked terrible and he felt even worse for forcing her to go out when she obviously wasn't feeling great. She'd mentioned morning sickness before, but he'd seen little evidence of it and, to his shame, had blithely put it to the back of his mind and forged on.

He thought about Ros's reluctance to go into the stable and his insistence that everything would be okay. Her frightened face as he'd encouraged her to come closer and give Ulysses his treat should have made him realize how uncomfortable she was in his world. It was an alien space for her and, if she was like that around horses, how much worse would she be around steers?

All of this brought home to him even more clearly how vastly different their worlds were. Hers was one of concrete and noise and skyscrapers and his was one of peace and animals and sky. They couldn't be less compatible if they tried. And yet, she'd agreed to stay here and have their baby. Agreed to at least try to make working from Royal a viable thing.

She'd made all the sacrifices and what had he done? Thrown a bit of money around, that's all. And that was no hardship for him. He'd given up nothing. Changed nothing. Guilt slammed into him. But what could he do? They'd made their bed and lain in it. He grimaced at the metaphor and the swift rise of arousal that escalated through him, but doing what he did best, he pushed it aside and went through to the mudroom and geared up again before heading out the back door. Outside, the air was still crisp and cold and he filled his lungs with the cleanness of it. This wasn't the fume-filled city. Here a man could breathe and dream. This was his life, his home, his everything. It clearly wasn't Rosalind's.

So where did that leave them? Would she stay? Or would she be gone the moment their child was born? A pang of loss struck him as he thought about Ros leaving. And while he told himself that, ideally, he wanted his child raised by two parents it wasn't mandatory. But the thought of losing her didn't sit as easily with him now as it had before their wedding. When they'd drawn up the marriage contract, he'd been adamant that any children born to them would be raised by him should their marriage dissolve. He had firm ideas about how he wanted his child or children raised and it would be with love and care and stability. Not the kind of careless and casual parenting his father had observed where he'd left everything to Gabe's mom and on those rare occasions when he'd taken Gabe out for a day all he'd done was splash money about and pass judgement on others.

That wasn't what Gabe wanted for his son or daughter. He wanted them to know they were loved and safe, always, and although it made him sound like a control freak and maybe even an asshole, the only way to ensure that was to have sole custody if his marriage didn't last. He refused to allow his child to ever be hurt, to be a part of a tug-of-war or be used as a weapon against their other parent. And he absolutely refused to be as absent and as cavalier about his child's emotional well-being as his father had been with him. But now the idea of not having Rosalind be a part of his life, together with the baby they'd created, made him feel an element of loss he hadn't experienced since his mother's death.

He shook his head at his thoughts. He didn't have time to dwell on maybes. Right now he had a day's work ahead of him and that's what he would do.

They fell into a routine after that. One where he did his work on the ranch by day, as she did hers inside the ranch house. Evenings they usually ate together before heading to their separate sleeping quarters. She'd taken to staying in bed in the mornings and he'd asked the housekeeper to take her tea and plain toast or crackers before she rose. She'd thanked him for it and admitted to feeling a lot better during the day if she just started slow. That was fine by him. She wasn't due to see the baby doctor for another couple of weeks and he planned to be right there along with her. In the meantime, it was easier to keep some distance between them because the more time he spent with her, the more time he wanted to spend with her and that wasn't part of his plan.

Gabe was in the stables, brushing Ulysses down after a morning ride when his cell phone rang. He didn't recognize the number on the screen and was tempted to send it to voice mail, but an edge of curiosity prompted him to accept the call.

"Gabriel Carrington," he said with a touch of irritation in his voice.

"Gabe, it's Rafael Wentworth. How are things going? Congratulations on your marriage, by the way."

Gabe smiled at the all-too-familiar voice. He and Rafael had been friends back in their high school days where they'd bonded over their mutual disgust with their fathers and, while they'd mostly lost touch after Rafe had left town when he was seventeen after a particularly tough time with his dad, they'd sporadically gotten in touch with one another. Rafe had made his fortune in Miami and had a bit of a reputation as a ladies' man. Despite that reputation, Gabe knew him as a man who, while always proud and ambitious, also valued integrity above everything else.

"Thank you. I saw you at the TCC gala, but with so many people, I couldn't get near you. I'm glad you're still in Royal. What's keeping you here?"

"I'm scouting out a new business opportunity."

"Have you seen your dad?"

"Briefly. But I've seen a lot of Cammie. That's a cute baby she's fostering."

"Yeah, your sister is doing a great job, although no one seems to know who the baby's daddy is."

"Well, despite the rumors filtering around the club, I can assure you it isn't me," Rafe said with a laugh. "In fact, I've pretty much had enough of all the rumors and questions. I've asked Cammie to organize a DNA test to prove that Micah and I are definitely not related."

"Good idea. Should stop the gossip train in its tracks. Say, why don't we catch up for a drink now you're back?"

"Sure, not the club, though. Too many ears for my liking at the moment. What about Sheen or that new place set up by Lauren Roberts…what's she called it?"

"The Eatery," Gabe supplied.

"Yeah, that's the one. Shall we meet there? Say, seven tonight?"

"I look forward to it."

They ended the call and Gabe found himself looking forward to catching up with his friend in person. It had been a while but if Rafe was back in town for good maybe they'd get to see one another more often.

Later that day, Gabe pulled up in a parking lot not too far from the restaurant and sprinted through the light rain to get there. He spied Rafe immediately over by the bar and crossed the floor to meet him.

"Good to see you, buddy," he said enveloping Rafe in a man hug.

Rafe clapped him on the back in return. "Good to see you, too. It's been too long."

"Well, I wasn't the one who left town."

"You weren't the one who had to," Rafe said with a crooked grin. "What can I get you to drink?"

"A zero alcohol beer would be good. Driving and all that."

Rafe gave his order to the bartender.

"So, what's brought you back to town?" Gabe said, taking a sip of his beer when the barman put the brew on a coaster in front of him.

"Cammie's nagging about the gala, but mainly it's a new business idea. Something I've been thinking about for a while but just need to find the right property, y'know? I never thought it'd be in Royal, but it's looking that way. How about you, still running the ranch?"

"Yeah, not a lot changes there. Although I've had some ideas about expanding it into more of an educational and training facility. Something to get city kids off the streets, out of trouble and into gainful and rewarding employment."

Rafe looked surprised. "That's quite an undertaking. What made you come up with that?"

Gabe shrugged. "Just an idea that pinged into my brain during my last trip to Houston. Seems to me there are a lot of disenfranchised youth about and not just in the cities. This might help set a few of them on a better path."

"That's philanthropic of you. What does the new wife think of all that?"

"Rosalind? I haven't discussed it with her yet. We don't really have that kind of marriage."

Rafe looked surprised. "What kind of marriage is it?"

"One of convenience, mostly. I wanted an heir and I needed a wife who wouldn't want all the messy crap that comes with relationships to help me achieve that goal."

Gabe grimaced. Stated bluntly it didn't sound very appealing or kind, which wasn't something that had bothered him before. So why did it now?

"Jeez, buddy, that sounds clinical. What happens if she falls in love with you, or you with her?"

"Not going to happen," Gabe said firmly. "It's a contracted agreement. She gets a financial boost to help her business out of a tight spot—I get my heir."

Rafe laughed. "You know how feudal that sounds, right?"

"I know but we went into it with our eyes open. I don't expect complications."

If that was so, why did he have to fight the urge to cross his fingers behind his back?

"Tell me about her."

"She's blond, petite, beautiful, has her own busin—"

"Not that stuff. What's she like?"

"Tenacious, she has to be to be successful in the fashion industry. She's also a city girl through and through."

"Doesn't sound like she'll fit on the ranch. Does she like animals?"

"Not as far as I can tell."

"Man, you'll have your work cut out for you. Your ranch is your life. I've always kind of envied you that. Being a man of the land and all. Even as a kid you always knew exactly what you wanted and went for it."

"What about you? And those rumors at the club? Has Cammie booked the test yet?"

"She's organized it all for me already. I damn well hate having to dignify the rumors but they've got to stop. You know yourself how these things get out of hand. Even though we were both in Miami, I never met Arielle Martin, Micah's mom. Apparently, my name is mentioned in some diary of hers and maybe she wanted to talk to me at some stage but I sure as hell never heard from her. I just want all the conjecture to stop. It's not fair on me but mostly it's not fair on the baby, either.

"I can understand why it's important he know who his daddy is but it isn't me."

"I get it," Gabe empathized.

Rumor and speculation had led his mom to the truth about his father's infidelities. It had been tough for her, a genteel woman, to continue to hold her head up after that. She'd always been proud of her position in her husband's life—proud of his achievements and her son's, of the life they'd built together. But all that had come crashing to the ground when she'd discovered everything that she'd held dear had been an illusion. She'd been devastated by the betrayal and seeing her like that had made Gabe even more determined to never hurt another human being that way.

Surely it was easier not to allow your emotions to become engaged than it was to try to piece yourself together when everything fell apart. Hell, even in his adult life, his own attempts at relationships had ended miserably. The last ending when he'd discovered Francine, his girlfriend and a woman he'd thought he loved and could make a future with, was cheating on him. It seemed he was just like his mother, too trusting and wanting to believe that others had the same dreams and aspirations as he did, when nothing could be further from the truth.

And Ros? He knew exactly where he stood with her and she with him, also.

Liar, his conscience whispered.

No, he slammed the door on that voice so hard the echoes reverberated in his mind. He cared about her because she was carrying his baby. It had nothing to do with attraction or love or anything complicated. Absolutely nothing.

Nine

Rosalind ended the call feeling a massive buzz of excitement. Things were looking up. The conference call she and Piers had just completed with a New York based retailer, who had stores nationwide, promised the lift their business needed. The company buyers had enthused over the samples Piers had couriered to them and were already talking about an exclusive supply contract. At this rate everything would be back on the same track it had been before the letdown in Australia. Better even, because the potential market reach here in America was so very much bigger.

She did a little happy dance across the living room of the master suite before coming to a halt in front of a hard unyielding male figure. Gabriel. Her body responded instantly and she felt her cheeks flush with color.

"Sorry, I didn't see you there," she said and stepped back.

"You look happy. That's good."

"Yes, I am happy. Piers and I just had a call with a company that will potentially be my biggest customer very soon. We just need to prepare the contracts and send them to their legal department."

"That's great news," he said, but she noticed his eyes didn't light up quite the way she was sure hers were.

"It means I'll be able to pay you back your money," she continued.

"That money is yours—it's part of our contract."

She pulled a face. The whole business of that marriage contract, and his subsequent withdrawal from any intimacy between them, had begun to make her feel like she was little more than a womb for hire. Sure, he was solicitous and ensured that her every need was met, but there was no affection or tenderness between them anymore. Even so, she found herself reacting to him every time he entered the same room she was in, as if just being in his presence heightened her every sense.

"What did you come to see me for?" she asked, rapidly changing the subject.

"I wondered if you were ready to meet my dad. He'll be visiting with my grandfather at the club later this afternoon. I thought we could call by for half an hour or so."

"Just half an hour?" she asked. "That doesn't seem a long time for you to catch up with your family."

"Long enough. I wouldn't inflict them on anyone any longer than that. They're..." he hesitated a bit, choosing his words carefully. "Very old-fashioned with their ideas. Don't be offended—it's just the way they are."

"That's fine—I've had to deal with people operating with outdated concepts my entire adult life."

"Well, I can only hope it will have prepared you for this, then," he said with a faint smile.

"What's the dress code? If we're at the club I imagine I'll need to do better than this." She ran her hands down the long, loose-fitting cream-colored woolen sweater she wore over a pair of camel-toned merino leggings that showcased her slender legs to perfection.

"You look great as you are and I hate to suggest something slightly more formal but—"

"What time do you need me to be ready?"

"Is thirty minutes cutting it too fine?"

She raised her brows at him. "I'll do my best."

She spun on her heel and headed for her bedroom and threw the doors to her walk-in wardrobe wide open. She had something in mind; she just needed to find it. Ah, there it was. The plain black crew neck knitted dress with its clinging long sleeves was perfect for a situation like this. It was the kind of thing that transferred well from office to evening wear with the mere addition of a few choice accessories and the right shoes.

Given they were heading to the club at this end of the day, she chose a pair of black pumps with slender heels and a twisted gold belt and matching necklace and bracelet to complete the ensemble. She assessed her hair in the mirror, deciding an updo would lend a little more gravitas to what she was wearing and swept the thick tresses into a sleek chignon before removing the light makeup she'd worn since this morning and applying a more distinctive eye-and-lip look. When she stepped back from the mirror she was well satisfied with her appearance. She only hoped she'd do Gabe proud.

Maybe if he was happy with her, he'd lighten up a little. She could understand that their marriage was essentially a business deal but he'd said he wanted their child to have a good life with two parents. But the way he kept shutting her out made her think that the whole concept was nothing more than a platitude.

She stepped back into their sitting room and caught Gabe sitting on the couch, leaning back with his eyes closed. Even though he was in repose, his face held unexpected lines of tension, as if he had a bad headache or, more likely, wasn't looking forward to the upcoming meeting.

"Everything okay?" she asked.

His eyes flicked open and he took in her appearance. "Wow, that's quite the transformation."

She did a twirl. “You approve?”

“Wholeheartedly.”

She’d never considered herself the kind of person who craved male attention and acceptance but knowing he thought she looked good was a balm to her soul right now. She’d begun to feel nervous about meeting the two senior Mr. Carringtons, but knowing she was okay in Gabe’s eyes went a long way to soothing her anxiety.

“Shall we go?” he asked. “You’ll need your coat.”

“Just a sec,” she said, nipping back into her bedroom and grabbing a white wool coat from her wardrobe.

It was a cape-shouldered style that folded over her chest and belted with a matching sash. Its wide arms had always made her feel like some kind of 1940’s glamor queen and right now it bolstered her confidence up a notch.

“Perfect,” Gabe said as she returned.

The trip to the club went smoothly and, on the way, Gabe peppered her with questions about her talks with the new client. Despite the fact his business was all about cattle and land, he had strong business acumen and she was grateful for his insights, which aligned very closely with her own. He seemed to understand her excitement and her desire to expand her business, not for expansion’s sake, but for the sake of her staff and their families, too. It felt like they were very much on the same page when it came to providing safe and encouraging employment opportunities. So why then were they miles apart on pretty much everything else?

Everything else but the bedroom, maybe.

What was with that? It was almost as if he was afraid to get closer to her. To her way of thinking, that would solve a lot of the tension between them. She knew she wasn't imagining it. Every accidental touch seemed to make him withdraw from her even more and even though he had a huge team of ranch hands and a manager, he was still very much hands-on and busy all day with the ranch itself. If she didn't know better, she'd say he was hiding from her, but surely that wasn't the case.

Her thoughts prompted her to ask a question.

"Gabe?"

"Hmm?"

"Just how hands-on do you plan to be with our baby?"

"What makes you ask that? You know I plan to be very present in their life." He sounded defensive.

"Well, I just wondered. You're out on the ranch all day long and I know as we come into spring your time will be even more eaten up. By the time summer and the baby come along, I was just wondering where we will fit into your day."

"Obviously I will make changes so I can be there."

She shook her head. "In the beginning maybe, but what about when it really counts. Like on the days the baby might be fractious or I might need a break."

"I plan to hire help—it is in our contract, remember?" he said, shooting her a frown. "Why are you asking all this now?"

"I'm just trying to clarify things. You want an heir, to be a dad, I get that. But there's more to baby rearing than simply popping in every now and then and leaving others to the mundane tasks."

"Trust me, I know how not to be a father. My own was a perfect example of that," he said with a quelling glance.

She let the subject drop but she couldn't help feeling that their expectations of their parental journey ahead of them were poles apart. She couldn't remember a time when her father hadn't been available to her. Even during his work with the diplomatic corps, he still made a point of being accessible. Her mom had quit work to be able to travel with her husband's postings and had been satisfied with creating a home wherever they went and acting as his hostess. But that wasn't the life Ros wanted for herself. Her career was important to her. Right up until she became pregnant, it had been everything.

Now she was going to have to find a new way of juggling her need to work and create and share her creations, with being a mom. Her need to excel at what she did would no doubt put additional pressure on her, but she'd find a way to come to terms with it. She had to. She settled a hand on her flat belly. It was still so hard to believe a new life was growing there. A life that happened due to chance. A life unplanned, unexpected, but cherished nonetheless.

They drew up outside the club and they left the car with a valet and went to check their coats in. Gabe took her hand and led her to the bar where they were meeting his dad and grandfather. The bar was tastefully decorated in modern hues but the influence of the past remained in the dark wooden floors and hunting trophies hanging from the walls. She suppressed a shudder at the many glass eyes staring at them as they crossed to meet two older men who stood as they arrived.

"Dad, Granddad, I'd like to introduce you to my wife, Rosalind Banks."

"What? Not Carrington? What's wrong with you, girl?" the older man barked before taking her hand to shake it.

Ros noted he only took the tips of her fingers and gave them the barest touch and the gentlest shake before quickly letting them go. It was the kind of handshake that always irritated her immensely. As if she wasn't an equal, or worthy of a decent handclasp.

"Pleased to meet you, sir," she said with a smile that belied the irritation that also arose at the expectation that she would automatically take Gabe's name. Then again, it wasn't as if he hadn't warned her. "As to my name, it's been good enough for me for thirty years, I figure it'll be good enough for at least another fifty or sixty."

"Hmph, would never have happened in my day. And he's got you knocked up already?"

"You'll have to excuse my father," the other man

said. "He has no social filter and tends to hold on to old traditions. He doesn't mean to be offensive."

Ros wasn't so sure of that but smiled and shook Gabe's father's hand anyway. At least he had the courtesy of actually clasping her hand firmly in the handshake.

"Pleased to meet you, Mr. Carrington."

"Call me Dad, or Denver. Welcome to the family."

"Thank you, Denver."

"What can I get for you both to drink?" Denver asked.

"I'll get the drinks. Same again for you two?" Gabe said. The two men nodded and walked on ahead as he turned to Rosalind. "Hot tea, or something chilled?"

She smiled and felt a curl of warmth in her lower belly. There was that solicitous side of him all over again.

"Tea, please," she answered.

He dropped his head to murmur in her ear. "Will you be okay with these two?"

"I'm sure I'll be fine. How much trouble can they get into in a few short minutes, right?"

"You have no idea," he muttered before heading to the bar.

Denver and his father waited for Ros to sit before resuming their seats. Denver leaned forward, his elbows on his knees and his hands clasped before him. Ros wondered if Gabe realized he had the exact same mannerism as his father when he sat and engaged in conversation with someone. Looking at the two older men was an interesting insight into how Gabe would age, too. No doubt he would continue to be a vital and handsome man for many, many more years yet, if his father and grandfather were anything to go by.

"Gabe tells me you make frocks?" Denver said with a challenging glint in his eye.

"Oh, I'm sure he told you I do a bit more than that," she said with an equally determined glint in her own. "Yes, my company does make special-occasion wear for women, but we're also well-known for women's leisure wear. In fact, we are on the cusp of branching out into the American market, which we're very excited about."

"You'll stop working once the baby is born though, right?" said Gabe's grandfather.

"No. I won't," she answered firmly.

"You're going to leave your child to be raised by strangers?" he persisted.

"Not at all. With a mom and a dad both working from home, there's no reason why we can't share our responsibilities."

"Hmph, never did that kind of thing in my day. Never saw why a man needed to do a woman's work. I s'pose you expect our Gabe to cook and clean as well after a hard day on the ranch?"

"Mr. Carrington, we do have a housekeeper and Gabe is quite adept in the kitchen. In fact, I think he enjoys cooking from time to time. We both do. We'll find our normal, I'm sure."

"Babies are woman's work."

"Well, it takes two to make them so I'm pretty sure that they benefit from two to raise them, too," she said firmly.

She was beginning to understand why Gabe had next to no idea of what was involved in baby rearing if his grandfather was any example. She had little hands-on experience when it came to babies, but even so she knew that it had to be easier working as a team of two than leaving everything just to one parent.

"You talk funny. You're not American, are you?" he continued doggedly.

"I have dual nationality, both American and Australian."

"Dad, stop misbehaving. You'll have Rosalind thinking we're from the dark ages," Denver interrupted.

"Gabe's gone and married the girl without a proper vetting from the family. A man needs answers to certain questions," the elder Carrington said gruffly.

"I'm happy to answer your questions, Mr. Carrington."

"Well, you can start by calling me Granddad."

"Granddad, then."

"Can you handle a horse?"

"No, sir—Granddad."

"What kind of ranch owner's wife can't handle a horse?"

"The kind who has never needed to or wanted to," Rosalind said, keeping a determined smile on her face.

"Dad, not everyone was born in a saddle," Denver said smoothly. "How long have you been back in the States, Rosalind?"

Grateful for the turn in direction, Ros quickly filled Denver in but was deeply grateful to see Gabe's return.

"I hope you haven't been grilling my wife in my absence," he said as he took the seat next to Ros and took her hand.

She squeezed his hand gratefully. "Not at all," she said breezily. "I was just telling your dad how we met in November."

A waitress arrived with a tray with their drinks. She set a small teapot and cup and saucer down by Rosalind, together with a small milk jug, then the whiskeys in front of the gentlemen.

"Tea? Oddest way to celebrate a wedding I've ever seen," Gabe's grandfather grumbled.

"You forget," Ros answered. "I'm carrying the next Carrington heir. It's my responsibility to ensure they get the best care and opportunity to develop that they possibly can."

"Humph." The old man looked at her and to her surprise gave her a wide grin. "You'll do."

"I beg your pardon," she said.

"What? You hard of hearing, girl? I said, you'll do. Welcome to the family."

Not even realizing how tense she'd been through the exchange with Gabe's grandfather, she felt herself relax.

"Well, I guess you'll do, too," she replied tartly and poured her tea.

The old man laughed out loud and winked at her. "I was just testing you. Sorry if I came across as unkind."

"No, just rude."

He roared laughing again and beside her she now felt Gabe relax, too.

"Right, now we have that out of the way, can we visit together like civilized human beings?" Gabe said dryly.

Talk quickly turned to ranching and without anything to offer to the conversation, Ros merely watched the interplay between the three generations of men. She drifted off mentally, until she heard Gabe suggesting that as Ros tired easily they would be heading back home. Ros didn't know whether to be grateful or annoyed that he'd made the decision without even asking her but she had to admit that she was tired and that the head-to-head with Gabe's granddad had taken more out of her than she'd expected.

They got in the car and headed toward the ranch but as the tires ate up the miles Ros couldn't help feeling that things were more off-kilter than they'd been before. She'd thought that maybe meeting with Gabe's dad and grandfather might bring them a little closer, make their marriage feel more real somehow even given their circumstances around getting hitched. Instead, it was as if the distance between them now stretched in an echoing chasm and she was at a complete loss as to what to do to resolve it.

She wanted this to work. She'd agreed to Gabe's terms but she wanted so much more. Was she destined to failure? It certainly felt like it. A real marriage involving intimacy, closeness, friendship and passion. They'd had intimacy and passion until Gabe had removed himself from that equation and now Gabe's behavior toward her was like that of a work colleague. She needed…more than that. For both herself and for their child.

But was Gabe capable of it? Having met his father and grandfather and seeing the examples he'd been led by, she seriously doubted it.

Ten

Gabe focused on the road ahead trying to remain oblivious to Ros sitting quietly in the seat beside him. Trying and failing. The subtle scent she wore seemed designed to torment him, to remind him of what it was like to bury his nose in the warm inviting curve of her neck where it met her shoulder. It made him want to do it again. But he'd chosen not to, he reminded himself firmly.

She'd leave eventually; he knew she would. Oh, she might stay a while for the baby's sake, but he knew this was not her world. She was like a butterfly needing color and stimulation, hopping from one exciting venture to the next. Life on the ranch was not like that, which made it easier to keep his feelings firmly locked in their airtight compartment, safe from harm. It was clear as day that she did not fit in his world and he would not risk having his heart dashed into a million pieces as his father had done to his mom when he'd left her. Unfortunately, that did nothing to alleviate the desire he felt for her.

He just had to try to keep himself clear of her as much as possible, which had been working since that episode she'd had at the stables. If anything, it had driven it home to him that he'd likely made the biggest mistake of his life that night they'd first made love after the gala. But it had led to what he hoped would be the best thing he'd ever done—created a child to love and cherish and raise to love the land as much as he did.

It was dark as they came up the drive, but even so, he knew what every shadow on the landscape represented. Every dip and hollow in the land, every fence line, every building. It was all his. He loved the ownership of it, the management of it, the challenges the animals and the weather brought him. And it would belong to his son or daughter after him. That had been his goal ever since he'd been a young boy and he was achieving it.

So why didn't it feel right?

He had no answer to that. When they entered the house, they went to their master suite and Ros went to take off her coat. He fought the urge to assist her, to peel the stylish garment from her shoulders, because he knew that if he did that, he wouldn't want to stop there. He'd want to go all the way, to slowly strip her naked and to lose himself in her. To wipe his mind clean of the taint he always felt after spending time with his father. But it wouldn't be right or fair to use her like that, even though he sensed she'd welcome him into her arms.

Gabe threw his coat on his bed and spun around and headed for the kitchen, determined to put some space between him and Rosalind before he did something incredibly dumb, like give in to his feelings. Feelings led to pain. How often had he seen that and been forced to learn his lesson? He didn't know if it was a curse on his family or not, but there hadn't been a single happy marriage in all the years there had been Carringtons in Royal. At least not one that he'd ever heard of.

All the way back to his great-great-grandfather, the Carrington men had been hard men of the land and focused on one thing: making money. And they'd been damn good at it. Womenfolk had been an accessory to a successful life and there had always been rumors of infidelity along the way. Rapidly hushed-up rumors, but they left their stain nonetheless. He would not be that person. He would not cheat on Rosalind but he would not give in to the allure that she presented to him, either.

A sound behind him made him realize he'd been standing at the kitchen counter for the past several minutes without doing anything.

"Everything okay?" Ros asked as she entered the room.

She was still wearing the black dress and he could not ignore the way it clung to every inch of her, highlighting the roundness of her breasts and the curve of her waist. She'd taken off the heels she'd worn earlier and was wearing a pair of slippers with an odd-looking animal on the tops of them.

"Are you wearing koalas?" he asked incredulously.

"I am. And they're a great deal kinder on my feet than the heels I was wearing earlier. My feet are oddly puffy this evening for some reason."

"Why didn't you tell me earlier?"

"Because it's just a little puffiness. No need to worry. By the time I get up in the morning it'll be all gone. Maybe you can give my feet a rub for me later on?"

He bit back the instant refusal that leapt to mind. Touching her, any part of her, would only lead to wanting her even more. But it was for her well-being, he reminded himself. She was the mother of his child.

"Sure," he answered abruptly. "Cookie has left dinner in the oven for us. Are you hungry now? We can wait until later if you'd prefer."

"No, I could eat now. Shall we take trays through to the TV room and watch a movie together?"

She started to move around the kitchen, gathering plates and cutlery and setting two trays before he could even respond. If theirs was a normal marriage they'd be dining together and watching a movie before retiring to bed—together. The realization sank like a stone in his stomach.

"No. I've just remembered I need to do some work in my office. I'll take mine through."

She didn't bother to hide the disappointment on her face. He hated hurting her like this—forcing more distance between them. But it was vital for his peace of mind. If he gave in, it would leave him vulnerable, weak. He could not be that person. Unable to look at her a moment longer, he turned and brought the covered dishes out of the oven, set them on pads on the countertop and lifted the lids. Cookie had done a potato gratin with green beans and a beef casserole with mushrooms that smelled like heaven.

"Shall I serve for you, too?" he asked.

"No, thank you. I'll take care of myself."

Her voice sounded small, as if she too had withdrawn emotionally from him and the situation they were in. He should be rejoicing in it; instead he felt a sling of guilt hanging around his neck. He could change all that in a minute, but he remained resolute.

"Here," he said, passing her a set of serving spoons and a ladle for the casserole. "You go first."

She gave him a weak smile of acknowledgment and scooped a small portion of each dish onto her plate. While she did so, he poured her a glass of sparkling water and added one for himself to his tray, too. Ros lifted her tray and turned to leave the kitchen but hesitated and turned back to face him putting her tray back on the counter top.

"Gabe, can I ask you a question?"

"Of course."

"Do you hate me?"

"No. What the hell? What makes you ask that?"

"It's just that you seem to be doing everything you can to create distance between us. I don't get it. You parade me out to your father and grandfather and then we get home and you're distancing yourself from me, literally. We're married. It's up to us to make the best of it. I know you don't want romance and all of that—I get it. And I accept that we entered into a contract. But does it have to be like this—so separate? Can we not find a happy medium somehow?"

"I don't believe there is a halfway, Ros," he answered gently. "I don't want to hurt you."

And he wouldn't let her near enough to hurt him, either.

She laughed and it was a bitter sound devoid of any implication of mirth or joy.

"You think I'd let you hurt me?" she said with a twist of her lips.

"Sometimes I don't think we mean to let others hurt us. Other times, we can't help but let it happen."

As he had with Francine before he'd decided on a marriage of convenience. Learning of her infidelity had cut him deeply. He, who thought he was more observant than his mom had been. More careful with his heart. Less trusting. Turned out it was those last two things that had driven Francine to seek another man's love and trust. The betrayal had cut deep but rather than devastate him, it had only served to make him more wary.

"You sound as though you're speaking from experience," Ros said carefully, giving him an assessing look.

"Both as an observer and as a participant," he answered and heaped generous portions of the casserole and potato dish onto his plate.

"*Participant*, that's a strange term to use for being in a relationship."

"It fits."

"It explains a lot."

He stiffened and gave her a hard look. "What do you mean by that?"

"That you don't see yourself as being partner *with* someone, but merely a contributor to a mutual joining."

Gabe shrugged. "I guess. Whatever, it doesn't change our position. I made it clear to you from the outset what would be involved. It's a little too late to be getting cold feet now."

His words sounded harsh, even to his own ears, but they needed to be said. She lifted her chin and stared at him with eyes that were now an icy blue.

"Who said anything about cold feet? I was merely having a conversation with the man I married. The man who is the father of my child. Is it too much to expect civility and friendship?"

She was gorgeous at any hour of the day or night but right now? With fury making her eyes snap at him and a flush of color in her cheeks? Well, she was stunning. His body stirred to unwelcome life but he wouldn't give in to desire. Desire led to emotional entanglements and with emotional entanglements came problems. He did not want to be hurt.

So, you'll just be bitter? A voice at the back of his mind said perversely. No. He wasn't bitter. He was careful. He would love his child, in fact, he did already. But he knew he could fall in love with Ros all too easily. Already he was drawn to her in ways he hadn't anticipated. Ways that would complicate things all too well when she left—and he knew she would in time. He'd seen her reaction to the ranch, the wide-open spaces, to Royal itself. Staying here was stifling her in ways he'd never considered. He couldn't expect that she would stay when it clearly was impacting her creativity and with that, her career.

She was the kind of creature who needed the buzz of bright lights and the big city. Something he'd never fully experienced or understood aside from the occasional visit to Houston or Dallas or a trip to New York to catch a show. While he hadn't minded the cityscape, he'd told himself it was only because he knew he didn't have to stay there. Didn't have to put up with the noise, the people, the smells. He would always have the chance to return here to clean air and to family.

Family. There was the rub. His mother was gone, he barely spoke with his father and his grandfather was cut from the exact same cloth as his dad. So maybe family wasn't what kept him here but now there would be a new generation. A son or daughter to raise to appreciate the land and the animals he farmed here, to teach the business side of ranching effectively—to love.

Was that what he truly wanted? Yes. It was. Someone to love unconditionally who would love him the same way in return. Someone he could trust—and who couldn't trust a child, right? They were a clean slate from birth. No preconceived ideas, no deceit. They loved without restriction.

He realized that while he was lost in his thoughts, Ros had settled at the breakfast bar and picked up her fork but was merely pushing her food around on her plate, not eating.

"Are you feeling all right?"

"I'm fine," she snapped. "You don't have to keep asking me that every five minutes."

"I wasn't aware that I did," he answered calmly.

"I'm sorry. I'm just out of sorts. I'm tired, I'm not hungry and I just feel so frustrated by everything."

He was at a loss for words. She wouldn't want any kind of placebo statement from him but he felt guilty that he had planned to leave her to her own devices this evening when she obviously would appreciate some distraction.

"Look, I can do my paperwork tomorrow. Why don't we choose a movie and eat in front of the TV like you suggested before?" he offered.

In response she pushed her plate away and got down from her stool.

"No, I think I'll turn in early. You do what you need to."

She tipped the contents of her plate in the trash and rinsed her plate before putting it in the dish-washer and leaving the room without a backward glance—leaving him standing there feeling all kinds of idiot. He hated that she had the capacity to do that to him, that he *let* her. It shouldn't have been a prob-lem to him. They'd both gone into this marriage with their eyes wide open and it wasn't as if she wasn't benefiting financially from the arrangement.

But he could see it was taking a toll on her. Bit by bit she was losing the vivacity and vibrancy that he'd seen in her from the first moment he'd laid eyes on her. And it was his fault. She'd been plucked out of her chosen environment and planted here on Texas soil—a place that was as foreign to her as the moon. Okay, so he hadn't forced her, but she'd been between a rock and a hard place. Her choices limited by the events that transpired after their first night of pas-sion together. Passion that was shared equally, as the result of that passion needed to be, too. Passion he was doing his level best to ignore.

She'd make a great mom, he realized with a twist of his heart. He only hoped he could be as good a father.

He picked up his plate and cutlery and forced himself to walk in the opposite direction of the master suite and down the hall toward his office. He would not go after her. They were married, yes, but that didn't mean anything other than a couple of signatures on paper. What was more binding was the contract they'd agreed to and he would hold up his end of that contract because he was an honorable man.

Honorable? When you let an unhappy, lonely, pregnant woman go to bed alone? There was that blasted voice again. He growled and kept going to his office. He would not give in. Giving in was a sign of weakness and he was not a weak man. He was not ruled by lust, as his father had been and still was by the ever-changing women who appeared on his arm, nor by love, as his mom had been. He was rational, sensible, loyal and hardworking. Not bad traits in any man, he told himself.

But as he settled at his desk and booted up his computer, he began to wonder what he was doing this all for. He ate his meal without tasting it and found himself studying the projections his ranch manager had emailed through to him without paying them the attention they deserved. In the end he closed his eyes and, elbows on the desk, rested his head in his hands while he massaged his temples.

This was supposed to be easy. Straightforward.

So why then was his mind in complete turmoil? Why then did every cell in his body urge him to go to Rosalind? To simply hold her. What difference would it make?

Every difference, he warned himself. It would be a sign of giving in to the weaknesses that destroyed his parents and he would not, ever, go there.

Gabe sat upright, shoved his empty plate away and forced his mind to the facts and figures on the computer screen. Everything looked promising for the development of his ranch into an educational facility. It would merely be a matter of applying for the right consents and then starting marketing and he'd be able to reach out to help disaffected and directionless youth from all around the region. Kids that needed a chance to find satisfaction in what they did all day, rather than fall victim to peer pressure and the trouble that boredom inevitably led to.

It was ambitious, this plan of his, but no more ambitious than what Rosalind had wanted for her own business. He grimaced, thinking about how he hadn't had to change anything in his life or his business and how she'd made all the sacrifices. He'd find a way to make it up to her, somehow, because while he didn't want to do marriage with all the usual trimmings, he didn't want her to leave, either.

Eleven

Rosalind woke the next morning still filled with a helpless empty feeling she just couldn't shake. She'd always exercised regularly until her move to Royal and knew Gabe had a well-equipped gym near the garage. Swimming had always been her preferred exercise but a brisk walk on a treadmill would probably help her clear the cobwebs away.

She dressed in leggings and a fitted long-sleeved T-shirt, both from her leisure wear collection and featuring a quintessential Australian print on the shirt, and went to the kitchen and grabbed a bottle of water from the fridge before making her way to the gym. Behind the closed door, music pounded out from the sound system inside. She hesitated at the door, her hand poised over the handle. The walls virtually rocked to the beat of Metallica at high volume and she couldn't help but smile. It was one of her favorite tracks. She opened the door and went inside and spied Gabe working out on a bench press. Dressed in shorts and a tank top, he exposed a great deal more skin than she'd been accustomed to seeing lately and by the way his clothing clung wetly to his skin he'd been at this awhile.

He was also oblivious to her presence and she took the opportunity to observe him, to relish the play of his muscles as they flexed with each press. He made it look so easy but one look at the weight he was pressing and she knew he was managing this through sheer strength and determination.

He completed one more repetition then let the bar rest in its stops and came up to a fully sitting position. It was then he saw her and she noticed the way his eyes sharpened as they raked her. Her breasts were fuller than they'd been before her pregnancy and while it was still such early days, she knew there was a new lushness about her figure that hadn't been there before. She took her time walking toward him, feeling a sense of satisfaction that he was so captured by her right now. But then the shutters came down on his gaze and he grabbed a nearby towel and wiped the perspiration from his face.

"Good workout?" she asked.

"Hard, but good," he replied before spraying the

equipment with sanitizer and wiping it down. "Planning to do some exercise?"

"It's something I haven't done enough of recently. I thought it might help."

"Help?"

"Clear my head."

He nodded. "I know what you mean. I've been slack lately. I feel like I'm getting out of shape."

Her eyes flicked over his body and the words blurted from her mouth before she could stop them. "Nothing wrong with your shape as far as I can see."

The air thickened between them and for a moment time stood still as their eyes met. Ros's body reacted instantly, a curl of desire warming and spreading from the pit of her belly, her breasts feeling fuller and tighter than before, her nipples hardening into taut points that became very obvious through her sports bra and the fabric of her top. Gabe's gaze dropped from her face to her chest and his nostrils flared as he noted her physical reaction to him. But then the spell between them broke as he shook his head once, abruptly, and, with a sound of disgust, snatched up his towel and walked away.

"I'll leave you to it," he said brusquely.

"You don't have to leave on my account," she called after his retreating form.

He muttered something indistinct, which she thought sounded a lot like, *Yes, I do*, and then he was through the gym's door and gone.

Metallica still boomed through the sound system in the gym and she left it going as she started on the treadmill. It suited her mood perfectly and helped her stay focused on her steps as she slowly increased speed and then incline. He'd said last night that he didn't hate her, but lately he couldn't wait to put distance between them when they were home alone. It was infuriating and it made her feel doubly lonely here.

Okay, so sure, she had no one living with her in New York, but at least there had been a bustling metropolis outside the door. She could go for coffee or a meal or to the park, or shopping—basically anywhere her whims might take her. But what did she have here? Land and cows? She shuddered. It would all be so much easier if Gabe would just allow them to be closer. Why couldn't they be friends with benefits? Surely it would have served to bring them closer as a couple, then as parents when the baby arrived. This yawning emptiness between them was driving her crazy.

It made her want to leave.

But she couldn't leave. She'd made a promise and she'd signed a contract. If she left, Gabe would have full custody of their child and all she'd have was visitation rights. A financial obligation hung between them that meant she needed to honor her agreement or face having to let her staff in Australia go. Just thinking about it made her feel sick to her stomach. Her staff were an extension of her family. They relied on her to keep work coming in so they all had jobs and their families had roofs over their heads and food on the table.

As awful as it might get here—and right now she felt pretty trapped—it was what it had to be. And she'd have to work her way through it. Maybe after spending some time sketching today, she'd go visit Miss Emmalou again. Ros knew the old woman was keeping something back. If she could befriend her, maybe she'd want to share her secrets with Ros, or at least unbend a little on the enigma that was Violetta Ford. Ros could see why that journalist, Sierra Morgan, was so fascinated by the story. The intrigue had her hooked as well, but first she needed to get showered and dressed for work and have some breakfast.

The walk on the treadmill had helped her mind to reset, though, and she felt like she was better prepared for whatever the day might throw at her. Probably cow poop, she thought with a wry chuckle as she stepped into the master sitting room.

"Care to share the joke?" Gabe said as he came through from his bedroom.

"Not really. You probably wouldn't appreciate it," she said smoothly and continued to her room.

She sensed him behind her but she continued walking and she could feel his affront coming off him in waves. So what, she decided as she firmly closed her bedroom door behind her. He was the one who decreed they should remain physical strangers in an affectionless marriage. To her mind that meant not sharing jokes, either. Okay, maybe that was petty, she conceded as she stripped down and stepped into her shower, letting the warm jets of water course over her body, but there was no doubting he wouldn't have found the joke funny and despite everything, she really didn't want to offend him.

Gabe was in the kitchen when she came through and he looked up at her for a moment before rising from the kitchen table and clearing his things away.

"You don't have to leave on my account," she said. "Again."

"I'm not," he said in that same brusque tone he'd used in the gym. "I have a meeting at the club. I'm not sure when I'll be back. Will you be okay on your own today?"

"You don't need to babysit me, especially when you've made it patently clear that you don't want to spend any more time with me than absolutely necessary."

"Look, I'm sorry about that. Obviously, I've offended you."

"Yes, you have."

There, she'd leave it at that and see what he came up with.

"Again, Rosalind. I am sorry. We blurred the lines when we consummated our marriage. We shouldn't have done it. It's…muddied things."

"Really? How? Are you afraid you'll fall in love with me or something?" she prodded.

His face froze into harsh lines. "I don't do love."

"Then I feel sorry for you, Gabe. You're missing out on one of life's best experiences."

"And its worst."

And with that, he stalked from the kitchen. Ros sank into a nearby seat, realizing she was shaking after the encounter. She didn't know why it affected her so deeply. After all, they barely knew each other. But she also knew that she was attracted to him in a way she'd never felt with any other man for that matter. She wanted to get to know him better, to understand him and, with time, maybe love him as she was sure he deserved to be loved.

Clearly his upbringing had been different from hers. So different that they obviously had strongly differing views on love. Who honestly thought that love was one of the worst experiences life had to offer? But it gave her pause for thought. If he couldn't see love as a good thing, what would that mean for their baby? Sure, he said he'd love and care for his heir, but if he didn't understand what love was, how fulfilling it was but how demanding it could be, too, then how could he be a good dad? What if he simply gave up when the going got rough, which it inevitably would. It was a sobering thought.

Gabe drove to the club with only half a mind on the road ahead of him. The other half was firmly trapped back at the ranch with a certain blond. He couldn't rid himself of the image of her in her workout gear this morning. She looked stunning in evening wear, as she had on the night he'd met her, and she'd looked knockout gorgeous yesterday to meet his dad and grandfather. But dressed in casual wear there'd been something elemental about her that called to him on a deeper level. As if she were some kind of siren and he an unwitting victim of her siren's call.

But he wasn't unwitting, was he? He knew what danger lay ahead if he went down that path and, despite her obvious attraction to him and his answering one to her, he'd removed himself from temptation and walked away. He should be proud of himself. But all he could think about was what it would have been like to close the distance between them and kiss her the way he craved. Kiss her, undress her and make love to her.

He growled out loud, immensely irritated by the train of his thoughts and how, no matter what he did, they always circled back to Rosalind Banks. And every darn time they did, he was left feeling out of sorts and physically uncomfortable. If he were a man like his father, he'd find an outlet for that discomfort. A willing woman who'd ease the demands of his flesh. But he wasn't that kind of man and, even more daunting, he doubted that it would make him want Ros any less.

Gabe was so deep in his own mind he almost missed the turnoff for the club but by the time he'd parked and walked through the entrance he'd almost convinced himself he had his thoughts firmly under control. The members' meeting itself was routine and, hanging around again like a bad smell, was Sierra Morgan. Gabriel wondered what it would take to make her go away. She had an unerring knack of pushing people's buttons while she investigated her stories.

Once the meeting was over, he sauntered to the bar area to order a coffee. While a few members began imbibing early in the day, Gabe was not one of those and as he waited at a table for his hot drink and a slice of pie, Sierra Morgan slid into a chair opposite him.

"Mind if I join you?" she asked once she was already seated.

He merely raised his brows at her.

The waiter brought him coffee but before he could take a sip, their attention was drawn by the sound of voices. Not loud, but certainly not in calm conversation, either. Gabe looked over his shoulder and spied his friend, Carson Wentworth, in a fierce discussion with his former opponent in the race for club president, Lana Langley. Words, like *bylaws* this and *rules* that, filtered to them before Carson made a dismissive gesture with his hands and walked away. Lana stared at him, obviously still seething, before turning on a high heel and heading in the opposite direction.

"Those two need to kiss it out already," Sierra observed. "Sparks fly whenever they're around—and not necessarily in argument, either."

"No way. Their families are mortal enemies. They've been feuding for generations."

"Mark my words. I'm right—you'll see. One of the things I've learned to be good at in this job is observing people and understanding what makes them tick. Those two, they're attracted to one another. They could make a concrete wall melt with all the energy they create when they're together."

Sierra rose from the table. "Better go. Stories to write."

After she'd gone Gabe took his time over his pie and ordered another coffee for himself, then asked himself why he was lingering here when he could be home working. But being home meant being in proximity with Rosalind and he wasn't sure if he was strong enough to continue to do that and not give in to the ever-growing urge to step into intimate waters with her again.

Why was it so darn hard to simply be together without the complications that emotions brought? He'd drawn his line in the sand and made his decisions. He didn't want love.

But suddenly the thought of an empty life stretching out ahead of him without it seemed a very long time, indeed.

Twelve

The next morning Ros followed the same pattern as the day before—to the gym for a brisk walk on the treadmill followed by some light weights this time, then shower and breakfast before settling in to work. Gabe was nowhere to be seen today and he'd been scarce all day yesterday, too. Despite the house-keeper's presence, the house pretty much echoed in silence.

Not wanting to spend another day completely alone, Ros drove into town after breakfast and browsed some of the stores. The range of goods you could buy was certainly varied, especially when it came to the baby, she realized as she entered a store that specialized in baby gear. Her hand hovered over a tiny onesie in pale gray with a baby elephant embroidered in white on the chest. She'd barely stopped to consider her pregnancy in terms of an actual infant, a tiny human being to love and to hold. Everything else around her had moved so fast from the moment she'd discovered her pregnancy, but right now the reality of her situation hit her hard.

She reeled a little, feeling slightly light-headed and put out a hand, but there was nothing there and as darkness consumed her, she fell to the shop floor.

"Are you all right, ma'am?" she heard one voice say close by her.

"Call an ambulance. Better safe than sorry," said another.

"Probably just low blood sugar—pass her a candy," suggested someone else.

Rosalind opened her eyes and struggled to sit up, only to be firmly encouraged to remain down.

"Don't rush up, honey, you fainted. How are you feeling now?" the first voice asked her.

"I'm okay. I just got light-headed and then..."

"Let me help you to a sitting position, then we'll see if you're up to standing in a minute or two."

The woman, about her own age, guided her up and requested the other two women hovering about to move away. After a couple of minutes Ros said she wanted to stand and the woman led her to a chair in an office out back and got her a glass of water.

"I'm Francine, owner of the store," the woman introduced herself.

"Rosalind Banks, potential shopper," Ros said with a wry smile.

"Oh, you're Gabe's new wife, aren't you?" Francine said.

"I am. Do you know him?"

"Oh, everyone knows everyone around here, and we were an item for a while."

Ros's gaze sharpened on the woman. She was certainly attractive. Slender and tall with shoulder-length glossy brown hair and dark brown eyes, she would have looked good with Gabe. And, from what Ros could tell so far, she had a sweet nature.

"I didn't know that."

"Well, our Gabe likes to play his cards very close to his chest. How's married life?"

"It's interesting."

Francine nodded. "I went out with Gabe for two years and I don't think I ever really knew him."

There was a wry note to her voice that made Ros sit up a little straighter and take notice.

"Well, we didn't exactly marry under regular circumstances," Ros said. "It was more of a business arrangement."

"I heard he'd hired some fancy high-profile international matchmaker to find him a wife. I thought it was just rumor. But is that how you guys hooked up?"

"No, actually, we met at the gala."

"And you hit it off straightaway?" Francine asked in surprise.

Ros thought of her physical reaction to Gabe the moment she'd seen him. It was a reaction that certainly hadn't dulled in the time since they'd met.

"You could say that," she said with a quirk of her lips. "It's why I'm here looking at baby clothes, after all."

"No kidding. Well, that's great news. I'm really happy for Gabe that he's finally getting what he wanted. We didn't part on the best of terms. I, uh, fell in love with another man while we were going out. Troy just swept me off my feet and I quickly realized that that was the kind of relationship I wanted. Oh look, here I am, hardly knowing you and just about telling you my life story. I'm sorry, that's all probably far more than you wanted to know."

Ros shook her head. "No, please, don't stop. I don't have any friends here yet and I'm feeling a bit isolated."

"Where are you from? I can't pick the accent."

"Sydney, Australia, but I had been hoping to settle in New York for a while, at least."

"And you ended up here?" Francine laughed out loud. "Girl, you have some issues with reading a map."

"Well, getting pregnant wasn't exactly on my short list of goals, but here I am."

"Gabe's looking after you, all right?"

"He makes sure everything I need is there for me," Ros said.

And it was true. She didn't want for anything in

a material sense. But physically, emotionally? That was a whole other story.

"But you're lonely, right?" Francine pressed.

"Yeah, I am."

"I was that way with him for two years and we lived together for twelve months of that. I kept thinking he'd change, that things would improve between us, but he's a closed book when it comes to his emotions. Happy to be part of a couple without actually *being* part of a couple if you know what I mean."

She'd hit the nail smack on the head. Ros nodded. "I don't really know what to do, to be honest. I thought I could do this, that my work would keep me busy enough that I wouldn't miss the rest. But being here and not really knowing anyone, well, it does make it all a lot harder and, well, Royal… It's not New York, is it?"

"No, it sure isn't. But look, you've made a friend today. I'd be happy to have coffee with you or do lunch. Not so sure Gabe would approve but who cares, right? You don't need his approval."

Ros smiled. "I'm glad I met you, Francine. Thank you for your help today and the conversation."

"Any time, Rosalind. Here, I'll give you my card and pop my cell number on the back for you. Call me when you need a chat or company. We'll work something out."

Ros got to her feet and was relieved to find she felt normal again. As she left the store she stopped and looked at the onesie again and resolved to return to buy it and a whole swag of other things for her baby. While its mom and dad might not have a traditional relationship, the baby would always get the best of everything else.

As she drove back to the ranch, she thought a bit more about what Francine had so openly shared. Gabe was an enigma, one she desperately wanted to unravel. A man of the depths of passion such as they'd shared was only living half a life if he wouldn't allow himself to love. Sure, sex had been great, but sex within a loving, caring relationship was another step above that and could help sustain a relationship for decades. Ros desperately wanted that with him and, with that realization, came to understand that even though she'd been unable to chip through his walls, he'd somehow inveigled his way through hers. She was falling in love with her husband. In itself, not a bad thing, but when it was complicated by the fact he wouldn't love in return, it made for a very unhappy future.

The hands-free function on her car rang and she answered the call. Maybe it was the prospective client in New York. She could do with some good news about now.

"Hello, this is Rosalind Banks."

"I heard you fainted. Stay where you are—I'm on my way to get you."

"Well, hello to you too, Gabe. How are you today?" she said with a touch of asperity in her tone he couldn't fail to miss.

"I was fine until I heard about you fainting. I've made an appointment for you to see the doctor and I'm coming to get you. Just tell me where."

"You can turn right around and cancel that appointment. I'm fine. I just got a little light-headed. That's all."

"Ros—" he started in a voice that told her he wasn't used to someone else countermanding his orders.

"Gabriel Carrington, I'm a big girl and I'm fully aware of the precious cargo I'm carrying. If I thought I needed to see the doctor I would have made an appointment myself. Now, stand down, big guy. Everything is fine. Besides, I'm nearly at the ranch and you can see for yourself that I'm okay."

He huffed out a breath of obvious frustration. "Fine, but if it happens again, promise me you'll get checked out."

"I promise. And how the heck did you find out anyway?"

"This is Royal, Ros. Someone heard from someone at the shop you were in and they rang me."

"Good to know the jungle drums are in full operation. I would have told you myself."

"Would you?"

"Of course I would. I wouldn't keep something like that from you. I'm just about home. See you soon."

She ended the call before he could say another word and she allowed herself to replay their conversation in her mind as she started up the long driveway to the main house. He'd sounded worried, frightened even. For her, or for the baby? She couldn't be certain, but given his emotional distance she had to suspect it was for the baby. Sudden and unexpected tears pricked at her eyes.

He'd been gruff because he cared. What would it be like to have that care and attention focused on her? Maybe, just maybe she could find a crack in that carapace he kept around him. He was essentially a good man and he was missing out on so much in life by keeping himself locked up like that.

Gabe was standing in the garage waiting for her as she pulled up in her stall. Dressed like a quintessential cowboy, he made her heart flutter and her girlie bits tighten on a swell of longing when she saw him there looking so strong and so concerned at the same time. She fiercely wanted him and she didn't know if that was pregnancy hormones or the fact that her feelings for this locked down man were escalating. The latter, she suspected.

He stepped forward and opened her car door, his dark eyes raking her as if to see if she'd been telling the truth about feeling okay.

"You're all right."

It was a statement, rather than a question.

"I told you I was." She got down from the SUV and grabbed her bag then reached up to cup his cheek with one hand. Operation Soften Gabriel's Heart started now. "I'm sorry I worried you."

She followed up with a kiss, pressing her lips to his with every intention of keeping it short and sweet, but the moment her lips touched his she was overwhelmed with the need to be closer to this complicated man. She let her bag drop to the floor and put both arms around his neck, the fingers of one hand spreading through his short-cropped hair. She felt the bolt of shock plummet through him at her touch, but then felt his body ease against hers, felt his lips begin to move in response to her kiss.

In seconds her body was on fire for him and judging by the hardness she felt at her groin he felt the same way. Why then couldn't they just keep going? But then she felt his hands on hers, gently pulling them from him as he lifted his face away. She could see it in his eyes; he wanted her every bit as much as she wanted him. His cheeks carried a flush of desire and his breathing was more rapid than usual.

"Ros, I thought we were clear on this," he growled.

"*You* are clear on this," she said stepping closer again. "I, however, am more than a little murky on the subject. Gabe, I want you. We are consenting adults. We made a baby together. Can't we please just let ourselves find joy in one another?"

He shook his head. "I don't want to hurt you. I won't love you, Ros. Not the way you want me to."

"Then let me take what I can get."

She kissed him again. This time tracing the seam of his mouth with her tongue and yanking at his shirt so her hands could slide over his belly and around his waist to his back. She put everything she could into the kiss. All the yearning she had for him at this point in time and somehow, some way, it worked. Suddenly she was lifted off her feet and then Gabe was carrying her swiftly down the hall and toward their master suite.

He kicked the door closed behind him and went to her bedroom in long strides, closed the door there also and put her down on the bed. He sat down and leaned over her, propping his arms on either side of her body.

"I will do this with you because you want it so much."

"You want me, too. I know you do," she insisted firmly, suddenly desperate to hear him admit it.

He looked conflicted, turmoil clear on his face and reflected in his obsidian dark eyes.

"Yes, damn it."

"Then say it. Say you want me."

"I want you."

She reached for him then, before pulling him down on her and wrapping her arms around him, kissing him with everything she had in her. He was big and solid in her arms and she reveled in the truth he'd finally uttered, the truth she'd ached to hear.

She kicked off the heels she'd been wearing and Gabe lifted his body from her. Seconds later she felt his hands at the waistband of her jeans. She raised her hips so he could slide them down her legs then sat up as he tugged her sweater and long-sleeved tee from her body. Her breasts spilled over the lacy top of her bra, her skin hot and flushed, aching for his touch. He stared at her as if he'd never seen her before, then ripped his shirt over his head, not even bothering with his buttons, before shedding the rest of his clothes and then rejoining her on the bed.

"You are temptation itself," he muttered as he traced the tops of her breasts with one knuckle.

She shivered under the gentleness of his touch.

"Trust me," she whispered. "I try my hardest."

She smiled and reached behind her to unsnap the hooks of her bra. It took a mere shrug of her shoulders for the straps to slide down her arms and the cups to fall away, revealing her full breasts tipped with dark honey-colored nipples. Gabe groaned and reached for her, his hands gentle as they cupped and kneaded her tender flesh before he bent his head and took her nipples, first one, then the other, in his mouth, rolling the taut buds with his tongue. Sensation speared through her, sending jolts of need straight to her core and making her wet and hot for him.

"Gabe?" she all but purred.

"Mmm?"

"Don't stop."

She felt his lips curve in a smile as he continued to pour all his attention on her breasts before slowly lowering her down onto her back. She clenched her hands on his shoulders, relishing the warmth of his skin and the strength of the muscles beneath it. He was a finely built man, every inch of him, and she was finding herself lost in tenderness. Surely this was their way forward. Surely he could not keep his heart locked away when they were so very perfect together.

She dragged her hands down the length of his back, sliding her fingers under the waistband of his boxer briefs and clutching his taut buttocks, holding him to her, against that part of her that begged for his touch.

"Patience," he said, his voice thick with desire.

"I don't want to be patient."

He lifted his head and cocked it, looking at her with lust-drugged eyes. "Are you sure about that?" he asked.

With one hand he cupped her between her legs, the pressure of the palm of his hand directly on her clit and sending a spark of intense pleasure through her. Pleasure she knew would only intensify the longer he spent giving it to her.

"Okay, maybe I do want to be patient," she gasped as he renewed the pressure on that sensitive spot once more.

"Glad to hear it, because I've a mind to take my time."

She laughed softly. "Then you do that. I'll just be your willing partner."

"I like the sound of that."

She did, too, but for a very different reason. For Ros, being his partner meant being his partner in everything. Not just housemates. Not just parents of their child. Partners in every sense of the word. Not that she could make him see that, just yet. But maybe, just maybe, he'd come to see it if they could rebuild the intimacy that had brought them together in the first place.

Gabe hooked her panties with his fingers and dragged the lacy garment down her legs before dropping it to the floor beside the bed. Then he let his fingers drift back up the length of her legs before resting at the tops of her inner thighs. She squirmed against the bed, wishing he would speed things up again but telling herself at the same time he was taking as long as he needed.

Even so, it was sweet torture as he kissed her thighs with little nips and strokes of his tongue to torment her even further. She pushed her hips up toward him, silently urging him to touch her at that point of her body where she craved his touch with a physicality that was making her mind unravel. And then, finally, he was there. His lips and tongue deftly touching and stroking. She was so ready that the orgasm that hit came hard and fast, a culmination of wanting him so much for what felt like so long and finally having him here in her bed with her.

Trembling in the aftermath, she eagerly reached for him as he moved up and over her body, settling between her legs, his hard length nudging at her entrance.

"I can feel the heat of you, your wetness," he murmured as he bent to kiss her. "Do you have any idea how sexy that is?"

"It's all because of you and what you do to me," she answered. "Do it to me some more."

He smiled and locked his eyes with hers as he pressed his hips against her, his erection sliding into her even as her body still clenched on aftershocks of pleasure from her climax. He began to move and Rosalind could feel her body responding again, felt the building swell of need and pleasure coalescing into a maelstrom of feeling. How was it possible he could do this to her? One touch, one look, and he had her virtually panting for him.

She needed him on a level that was daunting but right now he was exactly where she needed him to be. As the sensations building inside her reached their peak, she cried out his name giving herself over to the sheer wonder of their joining. Gabe, too, climaxed, his body rigid, driving deep within her as his own pleasure punched through him making him thrust inside her two, three, four times more. Her inner muscles tightened around him, holding him when he made to withdraw and she felt him shiver in response to her actions.

He wrapped his arms around her and rolled them onto their sides, holding her close. She nuzzled against his chest, inhaling the scent of his skin—a combination of the fresh soap he used, a light touch of cologne and the sexy maleness that was essentially his alone. Ros felt him relax, heard his breathing slow, felt his heart begin to return to a steady, less frantic beat.

"I love you," she whispered against his skin in a voice pitched so softly she was sure he couldn't hear it.

But the words needed to be said. In her heart of hearts, she knew that what they shared was so special she would never reach this level of bliss or this sense of connection with another man. Gabe was it and she was lucky enough to have found him. Lucky enough to be bearing his child. Now if only she could persuade him of that and encourage him to let her into his heart, too.

Thirteen

Had he heard that right? Gabe wondered, as he felt Ros's body soften as she drifted into sleep in his arms. He waited a few minutes and carefully extricated himself from the tangle of their legs and the loosening hold of her arms.

He put a soft blanket over her sleeping form and picked up his discarded clothing before making his way to his bathroom. He'd heard it right; he knew it. And it was his worst nightmare. He'd told her over and again that he didn't want to hurt her, but he wouldn't be able to help it now. Why had she gone and ruined everything by falling in love?

Love brought expectations and pressures he had no desire to yield to. He should never have given in to her coercion to make love. It had led to heightened emotion and a declaration he'd had no desire to hear. And it was his fault. He'd given in. Hell, he'd been so relieved to see she was okay when she returned from town, it was all he could do not to pick her up and lock her away in her room for the duration of her pregnancy. The idea of something happening to Ros had terrified him, gripping his chest with an icy hand until he could see for himself that she was okay.

He hadn't wanted to examine why it was so important to him that she be all right. It was simple biology, he told himself. She was carrying their baby and for that child, his heir, to come to fruition she needed to be well and safe.

They had to talk about this; they had to reestablish the boundaries of their marriage and they could not make love again. It opened up corridors that needed to remain firmly closed.

He stepped into the shower stall and turned the water to full cold, bracing at the shock against his body. Was he a madman, choosing this over curling up in bed with his wife? Some would likely say so, but given the words his wife had uttered this was the only response. He didn't shower long and was soon dressed and back in his office.

Hours later as he entered the kitchen he heard sounds in the formal lounge and, curious as to their origin, went to look. The sight that greeted him made his blood run cold. There was Ros, on a stepladder no less, arranging a string of fairy lights on a large artificial Christmas tree.

"What the hell are you doing?" he barked.

The instant he spoke he regretted it because Ros's attention came off what she was doing and went straight to him. The stepladder teetered a little, before righting itself, but that didn't stop him moving swiftly over the distance between them and lifting her down.

"Well, thanks for giving a girl some warning," she grumbled at him. "I was doing okay until you shouted at me."

"Do you have a death wish or are you just trying to be the death of me?" he retorted.

"Neither, I just wanted to put up the tree. I asked Doreen where to find everything. Christmas is just around the corner. I wanted to surprise you."

He felt churlish for having yelled at her but looking around the room at the boxes on the floor—boxes carefully labeled in his mother's clear handwriting—sent a shaft of loss and pain through him.

"Well, consider me surprised," he said bluntly and turned to walk away. "Stay off the ladder. I'll get one of the hands to help you."

"I can't get to the high points without it. Wouldn't *you* like to help me?"

"Frankly, I wouldn't care if you didn't put the tree up at all. I haven't had one up in years."

"But why not?" Ros asked, looking stunned. "It's

Christmas. I thought it would be fun for us. Our first Christmas together. Don't you celebrate?"

"No, but do whatever makes you happy."

He left her then, determined to put distance between them. A good hard ride might be what he needed to blow the cobwebs away and to prevent the memories of the last time he'd seen that tree and those decorations standing in his mom's front room. It had been the night she died and seeing them dragged out and the boxes open on the floor of his living room brought it all back again. The anxiety about her not being home yet, the darkening night, the unexpected snowstorm that blanketed the roads. The knock at the door by the police.

Gabe was at the stables before he realized he hadn't grabbed a coat or hat but he didn't care. He saddled Ulysses and led him out of the stables, swung up into the saddle and headed the gelding out to wider pastures. Several of his stock lifted their heads as he and Ulysses rode through, gaining pace the farther they got from the ranch house. It was only when he drew Ulysses to a halt that he realized that the reason why his face felt so chilled was because of the tears that had frozen on his cheeks. He scraped a hand over the evidence of his grief and vowed anew not to let her get to him, not to let her see the chinks in the armor that he'd so carefully constructed around his heart.

That tree, those decorations—all of them combined to remind him of one of the worst times in his life. A night made worse by the arrival of his father and grandfather and their platitudes and expressions of grief over the loss of his mom. Crocodile tears, all of it. If his dad had ever truly loved his mom, he'd never have treated her so badly, but then again, with the example his own father had given him, it was no wonder. Gabe had vowed then to never become like either of them.

Then why did it sting so much to realize how much it had hurt Ros when he'd refused to help her and had walked out? Hell, he hadn't even stopped to ask one of the guys working near the house to give her the help he'd promised. He turned Ulysses back toward the stables, the horse eager to head home in the cool air. At the stables he took care of Ulysses's needs before going back into the house.

He should apologize to Ros, maybe explain why he'd reacted that way, but wouldn't that lead to him having to open up about those messy things, feelings? Maybe it was better to simply keep his past firmly where it belonged. Locked up tight and never to see the light of day again. He went through to the living room only to discover the tree had been packed up and the boxes were gone. Everything was exactly as it had been when he'd risen this morning. Before he'd heard about Ros's fainting spell, before he'd driven himself mad with worry for her, before he'd made love to her with an intensity that had shaken him to his very core.

Before she'd told him she loved him.

He still had to deal with that. Nip it in the bud now. He'd already crushed her with the business over the Christmas tree, though. It would be like kicking a puppy when it was already injured to discuss her softly whispered declaration now, wouldn't it? But if he didn't face it down, didn't draw those lines in the sand, where would it lead? Would she too, like his mother, wounded in heart and spirit, make a fatal mistake one day? He couldn't let that happen.

He carried on down the hallway to the master suite. Her bedroom door was open and he could hear her moving around inside, humming a Christmas carol sweetly off-key. He pushed himself to go inside her room. The bed was still in disarray, a stark reminder of their passion earlier, but that wasn't what made his blood run cold. No, that would be the half-filled suitcase she had open on the bed.

"Oh, you're back," she said as she came out of the walk-in wardrobe with an armful of clothing. "I got a call from Piers and I wanted to share the news with you. My New York connection has connected. We're going under contract."

She sounded so delighted he knew he'd have to put this discussion on the back burner for now.

"That's good news, but why the packing?"

"I have to go and meet with my lawyer and we're having a joint meeting with the new distributor. The sooner the better. I've booked a flight out from San Antonio first thing in the morning and I thought I'd drive there tonight and stay over in an airport hotel so I can be fresh when I get to New York tomorrow."

"Weather's not great—I'll drive you."

"Oh, there's no need."

"Yes, there's need."

She shrugged and dumped her clothes on the bed before picking up individual items and folding and rolling them neatly before placing them in her suitcase.

"If it makes you feel better," she acceded. "I'll be glad of the company during the drive. You could stay with me in the hotel, too, if you like."

She took a step toward him and laid one hand on his chest with a mischievous glint in her eye. "In fact, *I'd* like that very much. We could revisit what we did together."

Gabe's entire body clenched. If theirs were a regular marriage, if she hadn't used a specific four-letter word—then sure, maybe he'd do that but given how she felt about him, he couldn't do that to her. He couldn't take from her what he wasn't prepared to give in return.

He put his hand over hers, forcing himself to hold strong and not to give in to the urge to agree to her suggestion. Even now, with her palm pressed against his shirt, feeling the warmth of her, it was so tempting. But he would not do it.

"No, I won't be staying." He lifted her hand away from his chest. "What time do you want to leave?"

"I'll be ready in about forty-five minutes," she said.

Her voice had lost a lot of the excitement that had shimmered from her only moments ago. He'd done that. He'd sapped her joy. And he had to bear the responsibility of it, too, along with the responsibility of getting them both into this lopsided marriage. He'd known when he met her that she was full of dreams and sunshine and fairy-tale endings, whereas he was the flip side of that being grounded in hard reality. He should never have slept with her, never gotten her pregnant, never married her.

But he'd done all those things and now she was a butterfly trapped in a glass case. Its beautiful, colorful wings batting helplessly and futilely against the barriers of its existence. He was that barrier. He took another step back from her.

"I'll leave you to your packing. Please, don't lift your case. I'll come and get it when you're ready to go. Have you eaten?"

Damn, he sounded like her mother again. Not like the man who'd brought her to two cataclysmic orgasms only a few short hours ago. He shoved that thought to the very recesses of his mind. It was not a good idea to go there. Ros rolled her eyes at him.

"No, I won't lift my case and, yes, I have eaten. Cookie made us something. Yours is probably still in the fridge. I'm assuming *you* haven't eaten?" she said with a supercilious quirk of her eyebrow.

"No, I haven't. I'll get on to that now." He started to walk away but stopped and turned and looked at her. "I'm sorry about the tree."

She shook her head. "No need. I should have discussed it with you first, I guess. This is your home, after all."

And yours too, he wanted to add. But it was clear she didn't feel that way and he wondered just how long this marriage of theirs was going to last. Not long by the looks of things. A sharp pang hit him in the chest and he rubbed his breastbone as he walked away. He'd been cold while riding out with Ulysses but that was nothing to the cold that permeated him to the bone, now.

She wasn't going forever, he reminded himself. She was attending business meetings and then coming back, wasn't she? Right now, he wasn't so sure and he had no idea of what to say to ensure she did return other than reminding her of the contract she'd signed. It wasn't as if he were offering her the love and affection she so clearly craved. Hell, he hadn't even let her set up a Christmas tree.

He muttered an expletive and retrieved his sandwich from the fridge. But he didn't feel like eating. Not when she was going away. Not when he was feeling all the things he'd been trying so hard not to feel. Maybe it was a good thing she was going to New York for a visit, he told himself. It would give him a chance to reset. To get his head straight. To maybe move to a bedroom in another part of the house so he didn't feel the temptation to stop in at hers every night when he went to bed.

He shook his head. He was a hopeless case. He

got up and put the sandwich back in the fridge before going to his office. Maybe he could do some paperwork in the time he had left before taking Ros to San Antonio. Whatever, he had to find something to distract him. Because his own thoughts were taking a very disturbing turn, indeed.

Ros sat down on the bed with a sigh. She couldn't understand the yawning chasm that had opened up between her and Gabe since they'd made love earlier today. He'd been so tender, so caring, so absolutely attuned to her needs. And then nothing. Nothing but coldness. Not so much as a speck of the warmth and passion they'd shared together.

She got up and went to her wardrobe, gathered a few more items to pack. New York was cold, colder than here, but she was certainly looking forward to going back. There was an energy about the city that she loved and the opportunities there were endless. She inserted the last items into her case and closed it before changing into a fresh set of clothing for traveling in. When she was ready, she went looking for Gabe.

Ros found him in his office, but he wasn't working. In fact, he was probably the most still she'd ever seen him. He'd swiveled his chair to face the window behind his desk and not so much as a hair on his head moved as he sat there.

"Gabe? I'm ready."

He started, as if he'd been asleep but when he

turned around, she saw that he'd been holding a photo frame.

"Who's that?" she asked, taking a step closer to his desk.

"My mom. Those were her decorations you were using today. She loved Christmas."

He didn't say much, but his words pretty much said it all and compassion bloomed through her.

"Gabe, I'm so sorry. I didn't mean to drag all that back up for you."

"It was a long time ago. I shouldn't have reacted the way I did. Maybe when you get back, we can do the tree together."

She nodded but the compassion she'd felt a moment ago was swiftly replaced by another emotion that was harder to define. She was sorry she'd hurt him, but if he didn't open up to her, how would she ever be able to avoid hurting him again? Before she could say anything else, he had risen from his chair and was walking to the door.

"Come on then, let's get on the road."

Ros followed him to their suite and then to the garage where she settled in his vehicle while he stowed the case in the trunk. He got into the car without saying a word and they left the ranch in silence. The silence stretched out between them for the entire duration of the journey and the longer it continued the less she was inclined to break it. There was so much unsaid between them and she ached to tell him again that she loved him, that everything would be okay.

But she didn't and, deep down, she didn't believe it would be, either. Maybe when she returned, they'd talk—really talk—but even the thought of how different they were and how differently they saw marriage still loomed between them. She was city and he was country. She loved bright lights, people and noise. He craved solitude, wide-open spaces and the sounds that came with the peace of the land. And despite all that, she loved him anyway.

She didn't know when she'd fallen asleep but she was stiff and her neck sore when she finally woke as they pulled into the front entrance of the hotel she'd booked.

"Gabe, I'm sorry to have slept so long."

"You looked like you needed it," he said and got out of the car.

She did the same and walked around the back where he was taking her case out of the trunk.

"Well, here you are," he said, standing back and looking more remote than he'd ever done.

A bellhop came forward to take Ros's case and she gave him her details, wishing he'd just go away so she could talk to Gabe. But what was there to say?

"Thank you for driving me. Are you sure you don't want to stay the night with me?"

His face hardened, looking as if it had been carved from granite. "No, thank you. I'll head straight back. I have a lot to attend to in the morning."

She nodded. "All right then, well, goodbye."

Ros stepped closer and reached up to kiss him but

at the last moment he turned his head slightly so her lips did no more than brush his cheek. So, it was to be like that, she thought with a disappointment that struck her so deeply she couldn't speak. Instead, she gave him a short wave and then followed the bellhop through the entrance. She didn't turn and look back, she couldn't, because if she did, she couldn't trust herself not to run back to Gabe and beg him to take her back to the ranch. She needed to do this trip. The future of her business hinged on it and with that the employment of all her staff.

Maybe when she came back, things would be different. But as she completed registration at the front desk and booked her ride to the airport for tomorrow, she knew that even wishing for things to alter between them was grasping at straws. Nothing would change, because Gabriel Carrington was exactly who and what he was. He hadn't pretended to be any different. She was the one who'd spoiled things by letting her heart rule the very practical arrangement they'd agreed on.

And she loved him.

Fourteen

Rosalind had felt different the moment she set foot in New York a week ago. It was as if the city sang to her, making her blood rush excitedly through her veins and her mind fill with possibilities. On the day she got back, her lawyer had collected her from the airport with a driver and begun discussing the contracts that had been proposed by her new client. Overall, it'd looked perfect and the first-stage payment from them would set her company back on an even keel. Everything had been signed late that afternoon.

She picked up her pencil and focused on the new drawings she'd begun this morning, because that meeting had ended up going so well, the new customer had also asked her for concept designs for an exclusive range for their firm alone. From where she was at the beginning of November, to where she was now, were poles apart. This was the life she'd craved. The ambition, the creativity, the hard work and the rewards. Everything she had worked toward since her very first design.

After serious discussions with Piers and the rest of her management team in Sydney, Rosalind had reached a decision. This was her home now, New York. It fed her soul in ways she couldn't even begin to describe. There was nothing for her in Royal. Nothing except a man who was incapable of loving her. It was an incredibly difficult decision to reach and it tore at her, knowing that her decision would create even bigger problems between them, not to mention the legal fight she had ahead regarding custody of their baby, but between his emotional distance and the stifled feeling she'd had living on his ranch, there was no way she could consider returning.

Aside from a Skype session with her parents, she'd spent Christmas Day alone with her thoughts and wondering about Gabe and what he was doing. Maybe things might have been different if he'd have been open to loving her in return, or even liking her enough that she could pretend it was love. She shook her head sharply. No, that was a ridiculous way to think. Why should she accept a half measure when she was prepared to give it all, herself? And even though it would crush her, she had to do this.

They'd always be bound by the baby she carried, and they'd have to find a legal way to deal with living in different states and co-parenting this life they'd created, but she was confident they could remain civil about it.

She looked at the old-fashioned calendar on her wall. He should have received the letter from her lawyer by now. It had been sent by express courier. She'd expected a call, an email, anything. But there'd been nothing from him at all. Maybe he was relieved she was gone. That way he wouldn't have to deal with her messy emotions or demands on him.

She pulled herself up. That was unfair. He wasn't born that way. The raw grief she'd briefly seen on his face when she'd found him with his mother's picture was evidence of that. Grief he'd rapidly masked, she remembered. Was that what it was that held him back from loving anyone? Had the pain of losing his mom been too much to bear? So much, in fact, that he'd shut himself off from the joy of loving anyone ever again?

Fifteen

Gabe turned the legal papers over in his hands as if he might see something different on the backs of the sheets. He'd been expecting it. There'd been an invisible divide between him and Rosalind when she'd left that he'd felt with a physical ache. He knew what she needed, but he knew equally well that he wasn't capable of giving it to her. Would it have made a difference even if he had, or would it have set him up for even greater disappointment if he'd loved her and she'd left anyway?

He shook his head. A contract between two consenting adults who were in agreement. It had all seemed so simple, but it had turned into a hornets' nest.

He missed her, as stupid as that sounded, and she'd only been gone a week. Who'd remind her to eat on time and well enough now? No, stop, he told himself. She didn't need a mother telling her what to do. She needed a partner, supporting her in what she did. She'd come to him as vulnerable as a woman could probably get and he'd taken the opportunity with both hands, capitalizing on it without compunction because it fit into what he wanted.

Deep down he'd always known he'd trapped a butterfly and he'd learned as a child that they didn't do well in captivity. He shook his head again. And here he was thinking about the ranch as if it were a prison when it had always been his life's dream to have his own spread and when his father had agreed to apportion half of the Carrington Ranch to him completely, he'd never once dreamed that he'd want to walk away from his dreams.

But he wanted to now. And why? Because he'd lost something that he'd seen as his? Could he ever have imagined that Ros was his completely? No, of course not. Especially not when he wasn't prepared to give her the emotional support she so clearly needed to feel at home in his life, too. She'd tried, he had to give her that. She'd given him the openings, the hints, the encouragement. But he'd been too bull-headed to listen to any of it. All because he hadn't wanted to get hurt or to hurt her in return.

And look how well that turned out, the voice in the back of his head jeered silently.

The phone on his desk rang, jerking him out of his contemplations. There was only one person who continued to insist on trying to reach him on his landline before trying his cell phone. His father.

"Carrington," he said tersely.

"Sounds like you need a drink, my boy."

Gabriel fought back a sigh at the sound of his father's voice. "I'm afraid if I start now, I won't stop for a few days," he answered honestly. "How are you, Dad?"

"Better than you by the sounds of it. Why don't you join me for a drink and dinner at the club tonight, say seven? I'll see you there."

His father hung up before he could refuse. The last thing he really wanted was to spend time in his father's company, right now. But what else did that leave him? His own? He looked at the papers he'd received from Ros's lawyer and made his decision.

"See you there, Dad," he said out loud as he replaced the phone in its cradle.

He set the papers on his desk. He'd deal with them tomorrow.

He looked at the gold ring on his finger and wondered if he should take it off. Was Ros still wearing hers?

At the club Gabe parked his car and went inside to find his father. Denver sat on his own in one of the bars.

"Dad," Gabe said in greeting as he perched on the chair beside his father.

"Son." Denver nodded to the bartender who brought two whiskies on ice. "Get that inside you," he said to Gabe as he picked up his glass and held it up in a toast. "To you and your blushing bride."

Gabe put his glass down on the counter without taking a sip.

"What's wrong? You two fighting already?" Denver said in a tone that teased but needled at the same time.

Gabe decided the easiest way through this was to just be up-front with his father. No point in fudging the truth.

"No, she's gone back to New York."

"Business or pleasure?"

"Permanently."

For a moment his father was speechless, not something Gabe had witnessed very often in his thirty-one years. Denver put his glass down on the counter, too, and swiveled to study Gabe carefully.

"You all right?"

Again, honesty seemed the best policy. "No, I'm not. And I'd rather not discuss it."

His father's face settled into serious lines. "You know, you could go after her."

"What? To drag her back by her hair, kicking and screaming because of a stupid contract? I have far too much respect for her to do something as archaic as that."

"Well, I wasn't suggesting that, exactly," Denver

said ruefully. "But why don't you go, talk it out, find a middle ground."

"What? Like you did with Mom?" Gabe shot back.

His father was hardly the man to be giving anyone relationship advice.

"I guess I deserved that," Denver acknowledged. "I'm sorry my choices made you so bitter, Gabriel."

"You treated her like an accessory to your life."

"I did, and it was wrong. We probably should never have married. I always knew what she wanted but I didn't think it mattered. My own mother had always been happy with her lot—I never expected any different when your mom and I married."

"How can you say you never expected any different?"

Denver shrugged. "I guess that's the lazy man's way out. I didn't want to face up to the fact that my decisions hurt your mother."

"Why the sudden turnaround? Your choices never bothered you before," Gabe said bitterly.

Denver sighed heavily. "I know it probably looked that way to you, but you can rest assured that I have had my own cross to bear with respect to my marriage. I had hoped that by staying away from you the way I did, it might give you a chance to be a better man than I was."

"I am a better man than you were."

Gabe saw his father flinch as if his words had been arrows flung straight at him.

"I deserved that and, yes, you are. I'm really proud

of you and all you've achieved, but you're just like me at the same time."

Gabe felt a surge of belligerence rise in his chest and he was that argumentative teenager who'd gone toe to toe with his father more times than he could count.

"No, I'm not."

"Then why aren't you following your wife?"

"Because she doesn't want me."

"Doesn't she? I know I said I am proud of you, but you know, you can be real dense sometimes."

"Dad, I didn't come here to be insulted."

Gabe picked up his drink and downed it in a few short gulps. "Thanks for the drink. I've lost my appetite for dinner so if you'll excuse me—"

"Don't you dare run away from me when we're having a conversation."

"A conversation? Sounds more like flinging abuse to me."

"You are so like your mother. Too quick to take offense and so guarded that no one can reach you when you really need them to. I bet that's what Ros did, too, right? Try to reach out to you, to touch your heart, and you kept it all clammed up like the bullion depository at Fort Knox. Any fool could see she was in love with you, not that you deserve it."

"I beg your pardon?"

"I said you're like your mother, and you are, but you're a lot like me, too. I didn't deserve her devotion or her love. I treated her as if she was an employee, not my wife. You, too, a lot of the time. I guess I just wasn't cut out to be a husband and a father the way a regular man is. But you still have the chance to fix that. Go after her, Gabe. Tell her how you feel about her."

"Dad, I don't even know how I feel about her."

"You do, you just don't want to admit it. Son, I let the right woman slip through my fingers by not being the man she deserved. Don't be like me."

As Gabe drove home later that evening, he replayed his conversation with his father in his head. They'd talked, honestly talked, for the first time in his life, and he'd found himself actually enjoying his father's company by the end of the night. Sure, none of that turned back time—it didn't bring his mother back, but it had laid the path to a new beginning with Denver. One not based on bitterness and recriminations.

So where did that leave him, he wondered. He had the ranch, sure, but while he told himself he needed it, his spread certainly didn't need him. He had employed the best of the best and the place ran like a well-oiled machine with or without him.

What did he really want? Rosalind. There was no question. But why? Had she inveigled her way into his guarded heart despite his best efforts to keep that part of him intact? He thought about his father's comment, about dying a lonely old man and it made his gut clench in fear. It didn't have to be that way.

All Gabe had to do was open up. To admit to his feelings for Ros. To love her the way she deserved.

This had to do with far more than the child they'd made together. He'd been drawn to her from the moment he'd first laid eyes on the sultry blond siren at the gala. He wasn't the kind of man to have a one-night stand. And yet he'd done so with her and the moment she was back in his life he'd done what he could to lasso her to his side in marriage. They could have still had an agreement to live together and raise their child together without marriage, but he'd wanted her tied to him in every way possible, even if he hadn't wanted to admit that to himself.

Could he do it? Could he walk away from the ranch, from everything he'd ever strived for and worked toward his entire adulthood?

Could he do it for love?

More important, would she let him back into her life?

Sixteen

Ros looked up from her design board at the kerfuffle going on in reception of her new workplace. She could see her new receptionist's back ramrod straight and heard her remonstrating with someone just slightly out of view.

"And I told you she's not seeing visitors today. What part of 'no' don't you understand?"

LaToya's hands went to her hips and, if anything, she bristled even more. Ros caught a soft Texan drawl, a voice she knew all too intimately. She dropped her pencil and walked swiftly to the door between her workroom and reception.

"It's okay, LaToya. He's my husband."

"You didn't tell me you were married," her staunch receptionist accused her.

If the woman weren't quite as good at her job as she was, Ros might have snapped a reply; instead she expressed her thanks for her excellent vetting skills and led Gabe through to her room.

"I suppose you'll be wanting a hot drink?" LaToya said following behind them.

"Thank you, I'll have my usual and Mr. Carrington will have coffee, black with one sugar."

LaToya snorted. "Man needs more sweetening, if you ask me."

She turned on her heel and disappeared in the direction of the kitchen. Rosalind closed the door to her workroom and gestured to the seats she had over to one side.

"That's quite the conquest you made there. Do you want to sit?"

She felt ridiculously nervous, skittish even. She hadn't expected Gabe to come all the way here and to turn up unannounced like this. She also felt that all-consuming tug that she'd almost managed to convince herself she'd forgotten in the days since she'd left Royal.

"Thanks," he said and folded himself down on the two-seater sofa she had positioned opposite two armchairs.

Her workroom at the top of a warehouse conversion was large and airy and the winter sun through the tall windows behind him bathed the room in a clear light.

"Nice place. You worked fast," he said carefully. "I didn't expect you to have space and staff already."

"In fairness, I had started the ball rolling before we married and LaToya is from an agency. I just hadn't expected to be working from here, myself."

An awkward silence fell between them and Ros had to force herself not to shift in her chair. He had come to her. She'd leave the floor open to him if he wanted to discuss the paperwork she'd had sent to him. LaToya came in with their hot drinks and set them down on the table between them, giving them each a hard look before raising a brow in question to Rosalind.

"Everything okay here?" she asked, looking fierce.

Ros fought back a smile. Her new receptionist knew she was pregnant and looked like she was prepared to eject Gabe personally if he was bothering Rosalind.

"Everything is fine, thank you."

LaToya sniffed and with a final glare in Gabe's direction she returned to her station.

Gabe looked at Ros with a puzzled expression on his face. "Did I say something to offend her?"

"Probably not," Ros answered. "She takes her role as gatekeeper here very seriously. That's all."

Gabe grunted. "Good to know you're surrounding yourself with good people."

"What are you doing here, Gabe?"

Damn, she'd failed at waiting him out but surely asking him directly was easier than sitting here, staring at him, remembering what he smelled like, how he tasted, what his skin felt like beneath her fingers. The sooner she knew what he wanted the sooner he could leave and the sooner she'd get back to work and her new normal, even if she knew she would always imagine him here, sitting sprawled on her little sofa, every time she came in. He had a way of imprinting himself onto her memory that was indelible.

She'd hoped she would have more time to inure herself to him before she saw him again. She'd hoped in vain.

"You're keeping well?" he asked, ignoring her question.

"I'm fine. Please, Gabe, tell me why you're here."

"I wanted to ask you out to dinner."

"What?"

"Yeah, dinner. You know, where people go to a restaurant, sit at a table, choose from a menu, get served their selection."

"Don't patronize me, Gabe. If you want to argue the terms of the dissolution of our marriage, please take it up with my lawyer. Now, if you haven't got anything else to discuss I really need to return to work."

"No, wait, please. I'm serious. I want to take you out for dinner. On a date."

"A date."

"We skipped a few steps. I thought I'd like to take some time to recover that lost time with you, if you'll let me."

She sighed sadly. "Gabe, it won't make any difference. You're still Mr. Texas and I'm Ms. New York."

"Humor me?" he asked. "Look, give me your address and I'll pick you up. Seven thirty? Eight? What suits you best?"

She stared at him a full ten seconds before answering. "Sure, fine, whatever it takes. Make it eight."

Ros gave him her address.

"Thank you. I'll see you then."

He swilled down his coffee. "Damn, she must have put half a cup of sugar in there."

Rosalind giggled in response. "I'm so sorry."

He shrugged and his lips quirked into a half smile. "I can change," he said before downing the sweet brew and placing his mug back on the table.

With that he left and Ros stared at his departing back, wondering exactly what he'd meant by that. Out in reception, she heard him thank LaToya profusely for the coffee before leaving their office space. The receptionist came back into Ros's workroom.

"That man all right in the head?" she asked.

Ros laughed again and it felt good. She couldn't remember the last time she'd found anything humorous.

"I'll have to get back to you on that," she answered

and lifted her cup of herbal tea. “Just don’t try any of that on me, okay?”

LaToya beamed in return. “Oh no, I like you.”

“Thank goodness for that.” Ros grinned back.

She was in a chronic state of indecision in the lead-up to eight o’clock. In the end she opted for the black wool dress she’d worn the last time she and Gabe had gone to the club together and accessorized with a blue patterned scarf that accentuated the blue of her eyes, and wore her hair loose. High-heeled pumps and sheer stockings completed the ensemble. She’d just slung her coat around her shoulders when the concierge buzzed up to say Gabe was waiting for her downstairs.

She let herself out of the apartment and took the elevator to the ground floor. Gabe waited for her in the lobby, flowers in his hands. The blooms were glorious and completely unseasonal, as if they’d been flown in directly from an Australian rain forest, in fact.

“You look great,” he said, stepping forward and passing them to her. “These are for you.”

“Thank you, they’re beautiful.”

The concierge cleared his throat. “Shall I keep them in water for you until your return?”

“Thank you, I’d appreciate it.”

Gabe led her out to a cab waiting by the sidewalk. He ushered her into the backseat and followed close behind before giving the name of the restaurant to the driver.

Ros was startled. The eatery, near Bryant Park, was popular and she thought the wait list to get a table there was weeks long.

"How did you get us a booking there and on New Year's Eve, too?" she asked.

"I know a guy who knows a guy," he said enigmatically.

"He must have some influence," she said in return.

"Actually, I went to college with the owner. I told him I needed to impress a girl and, hey presto, a table opened up for us."

She sat back in her seat and pondered his statement. Impress her? Why now? Why, when they were already married? They'd been there, they'd done that and they'd failed. If anything, living together had exposed all the reasons they shouldn't have married in the first place. What exactly was on his agenda?

They'd worked their way through appetizers and their main course and were lingering over dessert before she found out.

"Enjoying dinner?"

"Yes, very much. Thank you. It sure beats baked beans on toast."

For a moment he looked horrified but it dawned on him that she was teasing him.

"You got me, there," he said.

"I did, didn't I? Now, tell me, why are you here?"

He instantly looked serious. "I'm here because you're here. It's as simple and as complex as that."

She didn't understand. "What do you mean?"

"I mean Royal is a great place, but it's not home if you're not there with me."

She shook her head. "Gabe, you love Royal. You love your ranch. You don't love me."

He speared her with a look. "Don't I? Then why have I not been able to sleep since you've been gone? Why does every day stretch out before me like an interminable loop in time? Why do I miss you so much I can barely finish a sentence without thinking of you, wondering how you are or what you're doing? Sure, fine," he said, cutting the air with the palm of his hand. "That sounds stalkerish, I know. I'm sorry. But I can't help it."

Gabe drew in a long breath and exhaled just as slowly. "You see, I want to be where you are. I want to be your husband, in every sense of the word. To be by your side in everything. The good, the bad, the not-so-pretty. I want to be hands-on with our kid, not stuck out on the range working my guts out for some dream that I don't even want anymore. I need to be with you, if you'll let me."

"But what about the ranch? You can't just leave it."

"I can manage a lot of things from here just as easily as I did from there. I have a great team in place and the education center I told you about during dinner a couple of weeks ago is on track to begin in the spring. Obviously, I'd like to be there for the start-up and for each new intake, but I don't have to actually live there. Why would I when you're here?"

"But New York is nothing like Royal. It's crowded, it's noisy, it's go-go-go all the time."

"You know, I wondered what it would be like so I came here a few days ago. I've done some of the tourist stuff, but I've spent more time just walking. Feeling the city. Seeing what it is that drew you here in the first place. And I get it. There's a vibrancy that catches you here," he put a fist at his chest. "It fed something in me I didn't even know existed. But most of all, it's where you live and even if you don't want me back in your life full-time—just yet, or ever—I know I could make my home here. It feels familiar and yet so different from what I know all at the same time. It's wild and crazy and full of light and people, and it's solemn and interesting and has dark places and strangers, but all of it speaks to me in a way I never thought it would."

"You would run the ranch and the program remotely?"

"Pretty much. Pete is an excellent manager and he has a solid team behind him. Doreen is chafing at the bit to be a housemother to the youths we anticipate bringing to the property. To be honest, Ros, it'll be a win-win for everyone, but I need to know it'll be a win-win for you, too. You sacrificed so much to move to Royal and I was too stupid to understand that. Too stupid to see that your openness and your love weren't things to be afraid of, but things to cherish and protect. But now it's my turn—not just to make it up to you but to allow us to figure out what works for *us* and how we work together."

"But why, Gabe? I don't get it. Why are you turning your entire life upside down for me and our baby?"

"Because I love you. Because my world begins and ends with you and I don't want to ever live without you."

"But what if you find yourself to be a total fish out of water, like I did back in Royal."

"I won't. I know it deep in my heart that if I'm with you, and you're happy, I'm where I need to be. Look, I'm sorry I'm laying it all on you tonight. But it's my turn to try. My time to make it up to you for pushing you away. I had this grand plan of wooing you for however long it took to win you back and then asking you to marry me again."

"That sounds fun," she said carefully, still in a state of disbelief at what she'd heard from his lips.

Lips she ached to kiss again. She clenched her napkin in her hands to stop herself from reaching for him. How could she trust that he was telling the truth? *Isn't it enough that he's walked away from everything he knows to come to you?* Well, yes, there was that, she conceded.

"But how do you know you love me?" She cut straight to the chase. "You didn't want to love me before."

She couldn't help but sound accusatory. He'd hurt

her with his closed emotions. He'd pushed hers away as if they'd meant nothing and now he expected her to believe he'd had a complete change of heart? She said as much, fighting to keep tears from choking her throat and flooding her eyes.

"I'm sorry, Ros. So sorry. It was never my intention to hurt you. In fact, I held back because I didn't want to hurt you. I'd seen how my mother coped—or more importantly, didn't cope—when my father cheated on her. I'd seen how much she hurt and I remember all too well how I felt when I realized that neither of us was enough to keep him home. I saw my Mom risk everything for her love for him and he just threw it back in her face. I hated him for it—I swore I would never be like him but I had the awful sobering realization after you left that I have been no different after all.

"That fear of being vulnerable has colored every relationship I've ever had. I've allowed myself to become a victim to it, and it's left its scars. But I want to heal. I want to love. I want to live and not keep that vital part of me locked away any more. Look, I know this is a lot to take in, and it's a lot to ask. I'll give you all the time and the space you need but I'd like to ask you just one thing."

"And that is?" she asked as evenly as she could. It was no mean feat with her heart hammering in her chest the way it was.

"To give me, us, another chance. To let me love

you. To let me accept your love for me, if you still love me that is."

"Love isn't something you can turn on and off like a faucet," she said fiercely. "It consumes, it becomes everything."

"I know. I am consumed. You are my everything."

He said the words so simply, so without artifice and with such conviction she knew she had to believe him. She sat back in her chair and stared at him, noting the lines of tiredness around his eyes and the tension in every line of his body. He felt this, deeply and honestly, and he deserved honesty in return.

"Yes."

He blinked. "Yes?"

"Yes, I still love you. I will never stop loving you. But, no, at the same time."

His face, which had begun to glow with hope, froze. "No?"

"No, I don't want time and, no, I don't need space. I want us to be together. I want to be able to tell you every minute of every day how much I love you. I don't want to be apart. I want to know everything about you and I want to share everything about me, too. I want to start the New Year and every year after that with you, forever."

Gabe reached for her hands across the table. "I love you so much, Rosalind Banks."

"Rosalind Banks-Carrington, I believe," she said with a smile and a sense of joy that she felt rise from the tips of her toes and fill her entire being with light.

"I like the sound of that," he said. "Let's get out of here."

"I like the sound of that, too."

He settled the check and hailed a cab as they left the restaurant. The moment they returned to her apartment and they were inside her front door they were on each other. Hungry for one another as if they'd been apart for years, rather than days. Hungry to express in touch and embrace, exactly what they meant to one another. And when they crested the wave of their desire together, and the skies outside filled with the cascades of color from fireworks being let off all over the city, Rosalind knew she was exactly where she needed to be.

In Gabe's arms for the rest of her life.

* * * * *

Look for the next book in the
Texas Cattleman's Club: Fathers and Sons
series from
USA TODAY *bestselling author Jules Bennett!*

From Feuding to Falling

Available next month!

COMING NEXT MONTH FROM

HARLEQUIN

DESIRE

#2851 RANCHER'S FORGOTTEN RIVAL

The Carsons of Lone Rock • by Maisey Yates

No one infuriates Juniper Sohappy more than ranch owner Chance Carson. But when Juniper finds him injured and with amnesia on her property, she must help. He believes he's her ranch hand, and unexpected passion flares. But when the truth comes to light, will everything fall apart?

#2852 FROM FEUDING TO FALLING

Texas Cattleman's Club: Fathers and Sons • by Jules Bennett

When Carson Wentworth wins the TCC presidency, tensions flare between him and rival Lana Langley. But to end their familiy feud and secure a fortune for the club, Carson needs her—as his fake fiancée. If they can only ignore the heat between them...

#2853 A SONG OF SECRETS

Hana Trio • by Jayci Lee

After their breakup a decade ago, cellist Angie Han needs composer Jonathan Shin's song to save her family's organization. Striking an uneasy truce, they find their attraction still sizzles. But as their connection grows, will past secrets ruin everything?

#2854 MIDNIGHT SON

Gambling Men • by Barbara Dunlop

Determined to protect his mentor, ruggedly handsome Alaskan businessman Nathaniel Stone is suspicious of the woman claiming to be his boss's long-lost daughter, Sophie Crush. He agrees to get close to her to uncover her intentions, but he cannot ignore their undeniable attraction...

#2855 MILLION-DOLLAR MIX-UP

The Dunn Brothers • by Jessica Lemmon

With her only client MIA, talent agent Kendall Squire travels to his twin's luxe mountain cabin to ask him to fill in. But Max Dunn left Hollywood behind. Now, as they're trapped by a blizzard, things unexpectedly heat up. Has Kendall found her leading man?

#2856 THE PROBLEM WITH PLAYBOYS

Little Black Book of Secrets • by Karen Booth

Publicist Chloe Burnett is a fixer, and sports agent Parker Sullivan needs her to take down a vicious gossip account. She never mixes business with pleasure, but the playboy's hard to resist. When they find themselves in the account's crosshairs, can their relationship survive?

SPECIAL EXCERPT FROM

HARLEQUIN

DESIRE

Eve Martin has one goal—find her nephew's father—and her unlikely ally is hotelier Rafael Wentworth, who's just returned to Texas and the family who abandoned him. Soon, she's falling hard for the playboy despite their differences...and their secrets.

Read on for a sneak peek at
The Rebel's Return, *by Nadine Gonzalez.*

"I'm opening a guesthouse in town, similar to this, but better."

"You're here to check out the competition, aren't you?"

Rafael raised a finger to his lips. "Shh."

"That's sneaky," Eve said with a little smile. "I knew you had a motive for coming here."

He winked. "Just not the motive you thought."

She responded with a roll of the eyes. He noticed her long lashes fanned the high slopes of her cheeks. In the intimate light of the inn's lobby, her skin was smoother than he could have ever imagined.

Rafael was glad the tension that had built up in the car was subsiding. He wanted to make her laugh again, the way she'd laughed when they were alone in the garden. Her laughter had leaped out as if springing from a sealed cave. He'd wanted to take her in his arms and hold her close until she settled down.

"Incoming!"

Lost in the fantasy of holding her, he didn't quite understand what she was saying. "What's that?"

"Just...shut up."

She stepped up to him and brushed her lips to his in a whisper of a kiss. Rafael tensed, the muscles of his abdomen tightening. "Act like you're into it," she murmured through clenched teeth. With every nerve ending in his body setting off sparks, he didn't have to

HDEXP0122A

rely on dormant acting skills. He gripped her waist, pulled her close and kissed her hard, deep and slow. She gripped the lapel of his suit jacket and opened to his kiss. He heard her groan just before she tore herself away.

"I think we're good," she said, her voice shaky.

He was shaken, too. "How the hell do you figure?"

"I kissed you to create a distraction," she said. "P&J just walked in."

Paul and Jennifer Carlton were the most annoying couple in Texas, but at this moment he was making plans to send them a fruit basket and a bottle of wine.

"Here I thought you wanted to test that 'sex in an inn' theory."

"Stop thinking that," she scolded. "They're right over there. Don't look now, though."

He wouldn't dream of it. Her swollen lips had his undivided attention.

"Okay… They've entered the dining hall. You can look now."

"Nah. I'll take your word for it."

The manager returned with the keys to their suite, the one with the two distinct and separate bedrooms. The man was a little red in the face from what he'd undoubtedly witnessed.

Rafael plucked the key cards from his hand. "I'll take those. Thanks."

"Anything else, sir?"

"Send up laundry services, will you?" Rafael said. "And your best bottle of tequila."

The manager cleared his throat. "Certainly, sir. Enjoy your evening."

SPECIAL EXCERPT FROM

You won't want to miss
The True Cowboy of Sunset Ridge,
***the thrilling final installment of* New York Times**
bestselling author Maisey Yates's Gold Valley series!

Bull rider Colt Daniels has a wild reputation, but after losing his friend on the rodeo circuit, he's left it all behind. If only he could walk away from the temptation of Mallory Chance so easily. He can't offer her the future she deserves, but when he ends up caring for his friend's tiny baby, he needs Mallory's help. But is it temporary or their chance at a forever family?

"It's you, isn't it?"

She turned, and there he was.

So close.

Impossibly close.

And she didn't know if she could survive it.

Because those electric blue eyes were looking right into hers. But this time, it wasn't from across a crowded bar. It was right there.

Right there.

And she didn't have a deadweight clinging to her side that kept her from going where she wanted to go, doing what she wanted to do. She was free. Unencumbered, for the first time in fifteen years. For the first damn time.

She was standing there, and she was just Mallory.

Jared wasn't there. Griffin wasn't there. Her parents weren't there.

She was standing on her own, standing there with no one and nothing to tell her what to do, no one and nothing to make her feel a certain thing.

So it was all just him. Blinding electric blue, brilliant and scalding.

Perfect.

"I...I think so. Unless...unless you think I'm someone else." It was much less confident and witty than she'd intended. But she didn't feel capable of witty just now.

PHMYEXP0122

"You were here once. About six months ago."

He remembered her. He remembered her. This man who had haunted her dreams—no, not haunted, created them—who had filled her mind with erotic imagery that had never existed there before, was…talking about her. He was.

He thought of her. He remembered her.

"I was," she said.

He looked behind her, then back at her. "Where's the boyfriend?"

He asked the question with an edge of hostility. It made her shiver.

"Not here."

"Good." His lips tipped upward into a smile.

"I…" She didn't know what to say. She didn't know what to say because this shimmering feeling inside her was clearly, clearly shared and…

Suddenly her freedom felt terrifying. That freedom that had felt, only a moment before, exhilarating suddenly felt like too much. She wanted to hide. Wanted to scamper under the bar and get behind the bar stool so that she could put something between herself and this electric man. She wondered if she was ready for this.

Because there was no question what this was.

One night.

With nothing at all between them. Nothing but unfamiliar motel bedsheets. A bed she'd never sleep in again and a man she would never sleep with again.

She understood that.

PHMYEXP0122